"Steve needs you now, and he's going to need you even more," the man said.

The words hit her hard. Steve had never needed her. She had been too intense, wanting more from him, from their relationship, than he'd had in him to give. He'd always wanted a slight distance between them, mentally and emotionally, claiming that she'd "smothered" him. She remembered the time he'd shouted those words at her; then she thought of the man lying so still in the hospital bed, and she felt an unnerving sense of unreality.

Slowly she shook her head. "Steve is a loner. He doesn't need me now, won't need me when he wakes up and probably won't like the idea of anyone taking care of him, least of all his ex-wife."

She couldn't stay. She shouldn't. And she wanted to—more than anything in the world.

Dear Reader,

Each and every month, to satisfy your taste for substantial, memorable, emotion-packed stories of life and love, of dreams and possibilities, Silhouette brings you six extremely *Special Editions*.

This month, to mark our continually renewed commitment to bring you the very best and the brightest in contemporary romance writing, Silhouette *Special Edition* features a distinguished lineup of authors you've chosen as your favorites. Nora Roberts, Linda Howard, Tracy Sinclair, Curtiss Ann Matlock, Jo Ann Algermissen and Emilie Richards each deliver a powerful new romantic novel, along with a personal message to you, the reader.

Keep a sharp eye out for all six—you won't want to miss this dazzling constellation of romance stars. And stay with us in the months to come, because each and every month, Silhouette *Special Edition* is dedicated to becoming more special than ever.

From all the authors and editors of *Special Edition*, Warmest wishes,

Leslie Kazanjian
Senior Editor

LINDA HOWARD
White Lies

Silhouette Special Edition

Published by Silhouette Books New York

America's Publisher of Contemporary Romance

SILHOUETTE BOOKS
300 East 42nd St., New York, N.Y. 10017

ISBN: 0-373-09452-3

First Silhouette Books printing May 1988

Printed in the U.S.A.

Books by Linda Howard

Whether she's reading them or writing them, books have played a profound role in *LINDA HOW-ARD*'s life. She cut her teeth on Margaret Mitchell and from then on continued to read widely and eagerly. In recent years her interest has settled on romantic fiction, because she's "easily bored by murder, mayhem and politics." After twenty-one years of penning stories for her own enjoyment, Ms. Howard finally worked up the courage to submit a novel for publication—and met with success! Happily, the Alabama author has been steadily publishing ever since.

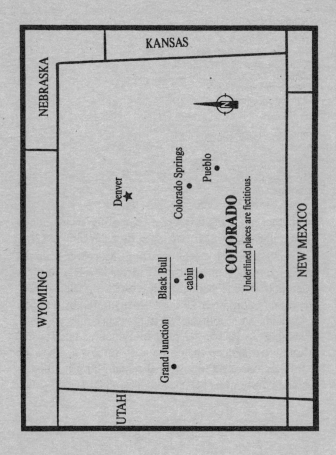

Chapter One

In ranking the worst days of her life, this one probably wasn't number one, but it was definitely in the top three.

Jay Granger had held her temper all day, rigidly controlling herself until her head was throbbing and her stomach burning. Not even during the jolting ride in a succession of crowded buses had she allowed her control to crack. All day long she had forced herself to stay calm despite the pent-up frustration and rage that filled her, and now she felt as if she couldn't relax her own mental restraints. She just wanted to be alone.

So she silently endured having her toes stepped on, her ribs relocated by careless elbows, and her nostrils assailed by close-packed humanity. It began to rain just before she got off the last bus, a slow, cold rain that had chilled her to the bone by the time she walked the two blocks to her apartment building. Naturally she didn't have an umbrella with her; it was supposed to have been a sunny day. The clouds hadn't cleared all day long.

But at last she reached her apartment, where she was safe from curious eyes, either sympathetic or jeering. She was alone, blessedly alone. A sigh of relief broke from her lips as she started to close the door; then her control cracked and she slammed the door with every ounce of strength in her arm. It crashed against the frame with a resounding thud, but the small act of violence didn't release her tension. Trashing her entire office building might help, or choking Farrell Wordlaw, but both those actions were denied her.

When she thought of the way she had worked for the past five years, the fourteen- and sixteen-hour days, the work she had brought home on the weekends, she wanted to scream. She wanted to throw something. Yes, she definitely wanted to choke Farrell Wordlaw. But that wasn't *appropriate* behavior for a professional woman, a chic and sophisticated executive in a prestigious investment-banking firm. On the other hand, it was entirely appropriate for someone who had just joined the ranks of the unemployed.

Damn them.

For five years she had dedicated herself to her job, ruthlessly stifling those parts of her personality that didn't fit the image. At first it had been mostly because she needed the job and the money, but Jay was too intense to do anything by half measures. Soon she had become caught up in the teeming rat race—the constant striving for success, for new triumphs, bigger and better deals—and that world had been her life for five years. Today she had been kicked out of it.

It wasn't that she hadn't been successful; she had. Maybe too successful. Some people hadn't liked dealing with her because she was a woman. Realizing that, Jay had tried to be as straightforward and aggressive as any man, to reassure her clients that she would take care of them as well as a man could. To that end she had changed her habits of speech, her wardrobe, never let even a hint of a tear sparkle in her eyes, never giggled, and learned how to drink Scotch, though she had never learned to enjoy it. She had paid for such rigid control with headaches and a constant burning in her stomach, but nevertheless she had thrown herself into the role because, for all its stresses, she had enjoyed the challenge. It was an exciting job, with the lure of a fast trip up the corporate ladder, and for the time being, she had been willing to pay the price.

Well, it was over, by decree of Farrell Wordlaw. He was very sorry, but her style just wasn't "compatible" with the image Wordlaw, Wilson & Trusler wanted to project. He deeply appreciated her efforts, et cetera, et cetera, and would certainly give her a glowing reference, as well as two weeks' notice to get her affairs in order. None of that changed the truth, and she knew it as well as he. She was being pushed out to make room for Duncan Wordlaw, Farrell's son, who had joined the firm the year before and whose performance always ranked second, behind Jay's. She was showing up the senior partner's son, so she had to go. Instead of the promotion she'd been expecting, she'd been handed a pink slip.

She was furious, with no way to express it. It would give her the greatest satisfaction to walk out now and leave Wordlaw scrambling to handle her pending work, but the cold, hard fact was that she needed her salary for those two weeks. If she didn't find another well-paying job immediately, she would lose her apartment.

She had lived within her means, but as her salary had gone up so had her standard of living, and she had very little in savings. She certainly hadn't expected to lose her job because Duncan Wordlaw was an underachiever!

Whenever Steve had lost a job, he'd just shrugged and laughed, telling her not to sweat it, he'd find another. And he always had, too. Jobs hadn't been that important to Steve; neither had security. Jay gave a tight little laugh as she opened a bottle of antacid tablets and shook two of them into her hand. Steve! She hadn't thought about him in years. One thing was certain, she would never be as uncaring about unemployment as he had been. She liked knowing where her next meal was coming from; Steve liked excitement. He'd needed the hot flow of adrenaline more than he'd needed her, and finally that had ended their marriage.

But at least Steve would never be this strung out on nerves, she thought as she chewed the chalky tablets and waited for them to ease the burning in her stomach. Steve would have snapped his fingers at Farrell Wordlaw and told him what he could do with his two weeks' notice, then walked out whistling. Maybe Steve's attitude was irresponsible, but he would never let a mere job get the best of him.

Well, that was Steve's personality, not hers. He'd been fun, but in the end their differences had been greater than the attraction between them. They had parted on a friendly basis, though she'd been exasperated, as well. Steve would never grow up.

Why was she thinking of him now? Was it because she associated unemployment with his name? She began to laugh, realizing she'd done exactly that. Still chuckling, she ran water into a glass and lifted it in a toast. "To the good times," she said. They'd had a lot of good times, laughing and playing like the two healthy young animals they'd been, but it hadn't lasted.

Then she forgot about him as worry surged into her mind again. She had to find another job immediately, a well-paying job, but she didn't trust Farrell to give her a glowing recommendation. He might praise her to the skies in writing, but then he would spread the word around the New York investment-banking community that she didn't "fit in." Maybe she should try something else. But her experience was in investment banking, and she didn't have the financial reserves to train for another field.

With a sudden feeling of panic, she realized that she was thirty years old and had no idea what she was going to do with her life. She didn't want to spend the rest of it making deals while living on her nerves and an endless supply of antacid tablets, spending all her free time resting in an effort to build up her flagging energy. In reacting against Steve's let-tomorrow-take-care-of-itself-while-I-have-fun-today philosophy, she had gone to the opposite extreme and cut fun out of her life.

She had opened the refrigerator door and was looking at her supply of frozen microwave dinners with an expression of distaste when the doorman buzzed. Deciding to forget about dinner, something she'd done too often lately, she depressed the switch. "Yes, Dennis?"

"Mr. Payne and Mr. McCoy are here to see you, Ms. Granger," Dennis said smoothly. "From the FBI."

"What?" Jay asked, startled, sure she'd misunderstood.

Dennis repeated the message, but the words remained the same.

She was totally dumbfounded. "Send them up," she said, because she didn't know what else to do. FBI?

What on earth? Unless slamming your apartment door was somehow against federal law, the worst she could be accused of was tearing the tags off her mattress and pillows. Well, why not? This was a perfectly rotten end to a perfectly rotten day.

The doorbell rang a moment later, and she hurried to open the door, her face still a picture of confusion. The rather nondescript, modestly suited men who stood there both presented badges and identification for her inspection.

"I'm Frank Payne," the older of the two men said. "This is Gilbert McCoy. We'd like to talk to you, if we may."

Jay gestured them into the apartment. "I'm at a total loss," she confessed. "Please sit down. Would you like coffee?"

A look of relief passed over Frank Payne's pleasant face. "Please," he said with heartfelt sincerity. "It's been a long day."

Jay went into the kitchen and hurriedly put on a pot of coffee; then, to be on the safe side, she chewed two more antacid tablets. Finally she took a deep breath and walked out to where the two men were comfortably ensconced on her soft, chic, gray-blue sofa. "What have I done?" she asked, only half-joking.

Both men smiled. "Nothing," McCoy assured her, grinning. "We just want to talk to you about a former acquaintance."

She sank down in the matching gray-blue chair, sighing in relief. The burning in her stomach subsided a little. "Which former acquaintance?" Maybe they were after Farrell Wordlaw; maybe there was justice in the world, after all.

Frank Payne took a small notebook out of his inner coat pocket and opened it, evidently consulting his notes. "Are you Janet Jean Granger, formerly married to Steve Crossfield?"

"Yes." So this had something to do with Steve. She should have known. Still, she was amazed, as if she'd somehow conjured up these two men just by thinking of Steve earlier, something she almost never did. He was so far removed from her life now that she couldn't even form a clear picture in her mind of how he'd looked. But what had he gotten himself into, with his driving need for excitement?

"Does your ex-husband have any relatives? Anyone who might be close to him?"

Slowly Jay shook her head. "Steve is an orphan. He was raised in a series of foster homes, and as far as I know, he didn't stay in touch with any of his foster parents. As for any close friends—" she shrugged "—I haven't seen or heard from him since our divorce five years ago, so I don't have any idea who his friends might be."

Payne frowned, rubbing the deep lines between his brows. "Would you remember the name of a dentist he used while you were married, or perhaps a doctor?"

Jay shook her head, staring at him. "No. Steve was disgustingly healthy."

The two men looked at each other, frowning. McCoy said quietly, "Damn, this isn't going to be easy. We're running into one dead end after another."

Payne's face was deeply lined with fatigue, and something else. He looked back at Jay, his eyes worried. "Do you think that coffee's ready yet, Ms. Granger?"

"It should be. I'll be right back." Without knowing why, Jay felt shaken as she went into the kitchen and began putting cups, cream and sugar on a tray. The coffee had finished brewing, and she transferred the pot to the tray, but then just stood there, staring down at the wafting steam. Steve had to be in serious trouble, really serious, and she regretted it even though there was nothing she could do. It had been inevitable, though. He'd always been chasing after adventure, and unfortunately adventure often went hand in hand with trouble. It had been only a matter of time before the odds caught up with him.

She carried the tray into the living room and placed it on the low table in front of the sofa, her brow furrowed into a worried frown. "What has Steve done?"

"Nothing illegal, that we know of," Payne said hastily. "It's just that he was involved in a . . . sensitive situation."

Steve hadn't done anything illegal, but the FBI was investigating him? Jay's frown deepened as she poured three cups of coffee. "What sort of sensitive situation?"

Payne looked at her with a troubled expression, and suddenly she noticed that he had very nice eyes, clear and strangely sympathetic. Gentle eyes. Not at all the kind of eyes she would have expected an FBI agent to possess. He cleared his throat. "Very sensitive. We don't even know why he was there. But we need, very badly, to find someone who can make a positive identification of him."

Jay went white, the ramifications of that quiet, sinister statement burning in her mind. Steve was dead. Even though the love she'd felt for him had long since faded away, she knew a piercing grief for what had been. He'd been so much fun, always laughing, his brown eyes lit with devilish merriment. It was as if part of her own childhood had died, to know that his laughter had been stilled. "He's dead," she said dully, staring at the cup in her hand as it began to shake, sloshing the coffee back and forth.

Payne quickly reached out and took the cup from her, placing it on the tray. "We don't know," he said, his face even more troubled. "There was an explosion; one man survived. We think it's Crossfield, but we aren't certain, and it's critical that we know. I can't explain more than that."

It had been a long, terrible day, and it wasn't getting any better. She put her shaking hands to her temples and pressed hard, trying to make sense of what he'd told her. "Wasn't there any identification on him?"

"No," Payne said.

"Then why do you think it's Steve?"

"We know he was there. Part of his driver's license was found."

"Why can't you just look at him and tell who he is?" she cried. "Why can't you identify the others and find out who he is by process of elimination?"

McCoy looked away. Payne's gentle eyes darkened. "There wasn't enough left to identify. Nothing."

She didn't want to hear any more, didn't want to know any of the details, though she could guess at the horrible carnage. She was suddenly cold, as if her blood had stopped pumping. "Steve?" she asked faintly.

"The man who survived is in critical condition, but the doctors are what they call 'cautiously optimistic.' He has a chance. Two days ago, they were certain he wouldn't last through the night."

"Why is it so important that you know right now who he is? If he lives, you can ask him. If he dies—" She halted abruptly. She couldn't say the words, but she thought them. If he died, it wouldn't matter. There would be no survivors, and they would close their files.

"I can't tell you anything except that we need to know who this man is. We need to know who died, so certain steps can be taken. Ms. Granger, I *can* tell you that my agency isn't directly involved in the situation. We're merely cooperating with others, because this concerns national security."

Suddenly Jay knew what they wanted from her. They would have been glad if she could have helped them locate any dental or medical records on Steve, but that wasn't their prime objective. They wanted her to go with them, to personally identify the injured man as Steve.

In a dull voice she asked, "Can't they tell if this man matches the general description of any of their own people? Surely they have measurements, fingerprints, that sort of thing?"

She was looking down, so she didn't see the quick wariness in Payne's eyes. He cleared his throat again. "Your husband—ex-husband—and our man are... were... the same general size. Fingerprints aren't possible; his hands are burned. But you know more about him than anyone else we can find. There might be something about him that you recognize, some little birthmark or scar that you remember."

It still confused her; she couldn't understand why they wouldn't be able to recognize their own man, unless he was so horribly mutilated... Shivering, she didn't let herself complete the thought, didn't let the picture form in her mind. What if it *was* Steve? She didn't hate him, had never hated him. He was a rascal, but he'd never been cruel or meanhearted; even after she had stopped loving him, she had still been fond of him, in an exasperated way.

"You want me to go with you," she said, making it a statement instead of a question.

"Please," Payne replied quietly.

She didn't want to, but he had made it seem like her patriotic duty. "All right. I'll get my coat. Where is he?"

Payne cleared his throat again and Jay tensed. She'd already learned that he did that whenever he had to tell her something awkward or unpleasant. "He's at Bethesda Naval Hospital in D.C. You'll need to pack a small suitcase. We have a private jet waiting for us at Kennedy."

Things were moving too fast for her to understand; she felt as if all she could do was follow the path of least resistance. Too much had happened today. First she had been fired, a brutal blow in itself, and now this. The security she had worked so hard to attain for herself had vanished in a few short minutes in Farrell Wordlaw's office, leaving her spinning helplessly, unable to get her feet back on the ground. Her life had been so *quiet* for the past five years; how could all this have happened so quickly?

Numbly she packed two dresses that traveled well, then collected her cosmetics from the bathroom. As she shoved what she needed into a small zippered plastic bag, she was stunned by her own reflection in the mirror. She looked so white and strained, and thin. Unhealthily thin. Her eyes were hollow and her cheekbones too prominent, the result of working long hours and living on antacid tablets. As soon as she returned to the city she would have to begin looking for another job, as well as working out her notice, which would mean more skipped meals.

Then she felt ashamed of herself. Why was she worrying about a job when Steve—or someone—was lying in a hospital bed fighting for his life? Steve had always told her that she worried too much about work, that she couldn't enjoy today because she was always worried about tomorrow. Maybe he was right.

Steve! Sudden tears blurred her eyes as she stuffed the cosmetic bag into her small overnighter. She hoped he would be all right.

At the last moment she remembered to pack fresh underwear. She was rattled, oddly disorganized, but finally she zipped the case and got her purse. "I'm ready," she said as she stepped out of the bedroom.

Gratefully she saw that one of the men had carried the coffee things into the kitchen. McCoy took the case from her hand, and she got her coat from the closet; Payne silently helped her into it. She looked around to make certain all the lights were off; then the three of them stepped into the hallway, and she locked the door behind her, wondering why she felt as if she would never be back.

She slept on the plane. She hadn't meant to, but almost as soon as they were airborne and she relaxed in the comfortable leather seat, her eyelids became too heavy to keep open. She didn't feel Payne spread a light blanket over her.

Payne sat across from her, watching her broodingly. He wasn't quite comfortable with what he was doing, dragging an innocent woman into this mess. Not even McCoy knew how much of a mess it was, how complicated it had become; as far as the other man knew, the situation was exactly the way he'd outlined it to Jay Granger: a simple matter of identification. Only a handful of people knew that it was more; maybe only two others besides himself. Maybe only one other, but that one carried a lot of power. When *he* wanted something done, it was done. Payne had known him for years, but had never managed to be comfortable in his presence.

She looked tired and oddly frail. She was too thin. She was about five-six, but he doubted she weighed much over a hundred pounds, and something about her made him think such thinness wasn't normal for her. He wondered if she was strong enough to be used as a shield.

She was probably very pretty when she was rested, and when she had some meat on her bones. Her hair was nice, a kind of honey brown, as thick and sleek as an otter's coat, and her eyes were dark blue. But now she just looked tired. It hadn't been an easy day for her.

Still, she had asked some questions that had made him uncomfortable. If she hadn't been so tired and upset she might have pinned him down on some things he didn't want to discuss, asked questions in front of McCoy that he didn't want raised. It was essential to the plan that everything be taken at face value. There could be no doubt at all.

The flight from New York to Bethesda was a short one, but the nap refreshed her, gave her back a sense of balance. The only thing was, the more alert she felt, the more unreal this entire situation seemed. She checked her watch as Payne and McCoy escorted her off the private jet when they landed at Washington National and into a government car waiting on the tarmac for them, and was startled to see that it was only nine o'clock. Only a few hours had passed, yet her life had been turned upside down.

"Why Bethesda?" she murmured to Payne as the car purred down the street, a few flakes of snow drifting down like flower petals on a light breeze. She stared at the snowflakes, wondering absently if an early-winter snowstorm would keep her from getting home. "Why not a civilian hospital?"

"Security." Payne's quiet voice barely reached her ears. "Don't worry. The best trauma experts were called in to work on him, civilian and military. We're doing the best we can for your husband."

"Ex-husband," Jay said faintly.

"Yes. Sorry."

As they turned onto Wisconsin Avenue, which would eventually take them to the Naval Medical Center, the snow became a little heavier. Payne was glad she hadn't asked any more questions about why the man was in a military hospital instead of, say, Georgetown University Hospital. Of course, he'd told her the truth, as far as it went. Security *was* the reason he was at Bethesda. It just wasn't the only reason. He watched the snow swirling down and wondered if all the loose threads could possibly be woven into a believable whole.

When they reached the medical center, only Payne got out of the car with her; McCoy nodded briefly in farewell and drove away. Snowflakes quickly silvered their hair as Payne took her elbow and hurried her inside, where the welcome warmth just as quickly melted the lacy flakes. No one paid them any attention as they took an elevator upward.

When the elevator doors opened, they stepped out into a quiet corridor. "This is the ICU floor," Payne said. "His room is this way."

They turned to the left, where double doors were guarded by two stern young men in uniform, both of whom wore pistols. Payne must have been known on sight, for one of the guards quickly opened a door for them. "Thank you," Payne said courteously as they passed.

The unit was deserted, except for the nurses who monitored all the life-support systems and continually checked on the patients, but still Jay sensed a quiet hum that pervaded every corner of the unit—the sound of the machines that kept the patients alive or aided in their recovery. For the first time it struck her that Steve must be hooked up to one or more of those machines, unable to move, and her steps faltered. It was just so hard to take in.

Payne's hand remained under her elbow, unobtrusively providing her with support. He stopped before a door and turned to her, his clear gray eyes full of concern. "I want to prepare you a little. He's badly injured. His skull was fractured, and the bones in his face were crushed. He's breathing through a trach tube. Don't expect him to look like the man you remember." He waited a moment, watching her, but she didn't say anything, and finally he opened the door.

Jay stepped into the room, and for a split second both her heart and lungs seemed to stop functioning. Then her heart lurched into rhythm again, and she drew a deep, painful breath. Tears sprang to her eyes as she stared at the inert form on the white hospital bed, and his name trembled soundlessly on her lips. It didn't seem possible that this . . . *this* could be Steve.

The man on the bed was almost literally a mummy. Both legs were broken and encased in pristine plaster casts, supported by a network of pulleys and slings. His hands were wrapped in bandages that extended almost to his elbows. His head and face were swathed in gauze, with extra thick pads over his eyes; only his lips, chin and jaw were visible, and they were swollen and discolored. His breath whistled faintly but regularly from the tube in his throat, and various other tubes ran into his body. Monitors overhead recorded every detail of his bodily functions. And he was still. He was so still.

Her throat was so dry that speaking was painful. "How can I possibly identify him?" she asked rawly. "You *knew* I couldn't. You knew how he looks!"

Payne was watching her with sympathy. "I'm sorry, I know it's a shock. But we need for you to try. You were married to Steve Crossfield. You know him better than any other person on earth. Maybe there's some little detail you remember, a scar or a mole, a birthmark. Anything. Take your time and look at him. I'll be just outside."

He went out and closed the door behind him, leaving her alone in the room with that motionless figure and the quiet beeping of the monitors, the weak whistle of his breathing. Her hands knotted into fists, and tears blurred her eyes again. Whether this man was Steve or not, a pity so acute it was painful filled her.

Somehow her feet carried her closer to the bed. She carefully avoided the tubes and wires while never looking away from his face—or as much of his face as she could see. Steve? Was this really Steve?

She knew what Payne wanted. He hadn't actually spelled it out, but he hadn't needed to. He wanted her to lift the sheet away and study this man while he lay there unconscious and helpless, naked except for the bandages over his wounds. He thought she would have a wife's intimate knowledge of her husband's body, but five years is a long time. She could remember Steve's grin, and the devilish sparkle in his chocolaty brown eyes, but other details had long since faded from her mind.

It wouldn't matter to this man if she stripped back the sheet and looked at him. He was unconscious; he might well die, even now, with all these miracle machines hooked up to his body. He would never know. And as Payne would say, she would be doing her country a service if she could somehow identify this man as Steve Crossfield, or as definitely not.

She couldn't stop looking at him. He was so badly hurt. How could anyone be injured this critically and still live? If he were granted a lucid moment, right now, would he even want to live? Would he be able to walk again? Use his hands? See? Think? Or would he take stock of his injuries and tell the doctors, "Thanks, guys, but I think I'll take my chances at the Pearly Gates."

But perhaps he had a tremendous will to live. Perhaps that was what had kept him alive this long, an unconscious, deep-seated will to *be*. Fierce determination could move mountains.

Hesitantly she stretched out her hand and touched his right arm, just above the bandages that covered his burns. His skin was hot to the touch, and she jerked her fingers back in surprise. Somehow she had thought he would be cold. This intense heat was another sign of how brightly life still burned inside him, despite his stillness. Slowly her hand returned to his arm, lightly resting on the smooth skin just below the inside of his elbow, taking care not to disturb the IV needle that dripped a clear liquid into a vein.

He was warm. He was alive.

Her heart was pounding in her chest, some intense emotion welling up in her until she thought she would burst from the effort of trying to control it. It staggered her to think of what he had been through, yet he was still fighting, defying the odds, his spirit too fierce and proud to just let go. If she could have, she would have suffered the pain in his place.

And his body had been invaded enough. Needles pierced his veins; wire and electrodes picked up and broadcast his every heartbeat. As if he didn't have enough wounds already, the doctors had made more to insert drainage tubes in his chest and side, and there were other tubes, as well. Every day a host of strangers looked at him and treated him as if he were nothing but a slab of meat, all to save his life.

But she wouldn't invade his privacy, not in this manner. Modesty might not mean anything to him, but it was still his choice to make.

All her attention was focused on him; nothing else in the world existed in this moment except the man lying so still in the hospital bed. Was this Steve? Would she feel some sense of familiarity, despite the disfiguring swelling and the bandages that swathed him? She tried to remember.

Had Steve been this muscular? Had his arms been this thick, his chest this deep? He could have changed, gained weight, done a lot of physical work that would have developed his shoulders and arms more, so she couldn't go by that. Men got heavier in the chest as they matured.

His chest had been shaved. She looked at the dark stubble of body hair. Steve had had chest hair, though not a lot of it.

His beard? She looked at his jaw, what she could see of it, but his face was so swollen that she couldn't find anything familiar. Even his lips were swollen.

Something wet trickled down her cheek, and in surprise she dashed her hand across her face. She hadn't even realized she was crying.

Payne reentered the room and silently offered her his handkerchief. When she had wiped her face he led her away from the bedside, his arm warm and comforting around her waist, letting her lean on him. "I'm sorry," he finally offered. "I know it isn't easy."

She shook her head, feeling like a fool for breaking down like that, especially in light of what she had to tell him. "I don't know. I'm sorry, but I can't tell if he's Steve, or not. I just . . . can't."

"Do you think he could be?" Payne asked insistently.

Jay rubbed her temples. "I suppose so. I can't *tell*. There are so many bandages—"

"I understand. I know how difficult it is. But I need something to tell my superiors. Was your husband that tall? Was there anything at all familiar about him?"

If he understood, why did he keep pushing? Her headache was getting worse by the second. "I just don't know!" she cried. "I guess Steve is that tall, but it's hard to tell when he's lying down. Steve has dark hair and brown eyes, but I can't even tell that much about this man!"

Payne looked down at her. "It's on his medical sheet," he said quietly. "Brown hair and brown eyes."

For a moment the import of that didn't register; then her eyes widened. She hadn't felt any sense of recognition for the man at all, but she was still dazed by the storm of emotion he *had* caused in her: pity, yes, but also awe, that he was still alive and fighting, and an almost staggering respect for the determination and sheer guts he must have.

Very faintly, her face white, she said, "Then he must be Steve, mustn't he?"

A flash of relief crossed Payne's face, then was gone before she could be certain it was there. He nodded. "I'll notify our people that you've verified his identity. He's Steve Crossfield."

Chapter Two

When Jay awoke the next morning she lay very still in the bed, staring around the unfamiliar hotel room and trying to orient herself. The events of the previous day were mostly a blur, except for the crystal-clear memory she had of the injured man in the hospital. Steve. That man was Steve.

She should have recognized him. Even though it had been five years, she had once loved him. *Something* about him should have been familiar, despite the disfiguring bruises and swelling. An odd feeling of guilt assailed her, though she knew it was ridiculous, but it was as if she had let him down somehow, reduced him to the level of being too unimportant in her life for her to remember how he looked.

Grimacing, Jay got out of bed. There she went again, letting things matter too much to her. Steve had constantly told her to lighten up, and his tone had sometimes been full of impatience. That was another area where they had been incompatible. She was too intense, too involved with everyday life and the world around her, while Steve had skated blithely on the surface.

She was free to return to New York that morning, but she was reluctant to do so. It was only Saturday; there was no hurry as long as she returned in time to go to work Monday morning. She didn't want to sit in her apartment all weekend long and brood about being unemployed, and she wanted to see Steve again. That seemed to be what Payne wanted, too. He hadn't mentioned making arrangements for her return to New York.

She had been so exhausted that for once she had slept deeply, and as a result the shadows beneath her eyes weren't as dark as they usually were. She stared into the bathroom mirror, wondering if being fired might have been a blessing in disguise. The way she had been pushing herself had been hard on her health, burning away weight she couldn't afford to lose, drawing the skin tightly over her facial bones so that she looked both haggard and emaciated, especially without makeup. She made a face at herself in the mirror. She'd never been a beauty and never would be, but she had once been pretty. Her dark blue eyes and swath of sleek, heavy, golden-honey-brown hair were her best features, though the rest of her face could be described as ordinary.

What would Steve say if he could see her now? Would he be disappointed, and bluntly say so?

Why couldn't she get him out of her mind? It was natural to be concerned about him, to feel sharp sympathy because of his terrible injuries, but she couldn't stop herself from wondering what he would think, what he would say, about her. Not the Steve he had been before, that charming but unreliable will-o'-the-wisp, but the man he was now: harder, stronger, with the fierce will to survive that had kept him alive in the face of overwhelming odds. What would that man think of her? Would he still want her?

The thought made her face flame, and she jerked away from the mirror to turn on the shower. She must be going mad! He was an invalid. Even now, it wasn't by any means certain that he would survive, despite his fighting nature. And even if he did, he might not function as well as he had before. The surgery to save his sight might not have worked; they wouldn't know until the bandages came off. He might have brain damage. He might not be able to walk, talk or feed himself.

Helplessly she felt hot tears begin to slide down her cheeks again. Why should she cry for him now? Why couldn't she stop crying for him? Every time she thought of him she started crying, which was ridiculous, when she hadn't even been able to recognize him.

Payne was calling for her at ten, so she forced herself to stop crying and get ready. She managed that with plenty of time to spare, then found, surprisingly, that she was hungry. She usually didn't eat breakfast, sustaining herself with an endless supply of coffee until lunch, when her stomach would be burning and she wouldn't be able to eat much. But already the strain of her job was fading away, and she wanted food.

She ordered breakfast from room service and received it in a startlingly short length of time. Falling on the tray like a famine victim, she devoured the omelet and toast in record time; when Payne knocked on her door, she had been finished for almost half an hour.

Without seeming to, Payne studied her face with sharp eyes that noted and analyzed every detail. She'd been crying. This was really getting to her, and though that was exactly what they wanted, he still regretted that she had to be hurt. She also looked immeasurably better this morning, with a bit of color in her face. Her marvelous eyes were bigger and brighter than he had remembered, but part of that was the result of her tears. He only hoped she wouldn't have to shed too many more.

"I've already called to check on his condition," he reported, taking her arm. "Good news. His vital signs are improving. He's still unconscious, but his brain waves are increasing in activity and the doctors are more optimistic than they've been. He's really done better than anyone expected."

She didn't point out that they had expected him to die, so anything was better than that. She didn't want to think about how close he had come to dying. In some way she didn't understand, Steve had become too important to her during those minutes when she had stood beside his bed and touched his arm.

The big white naval hospital was much busier that morning than it had been the night before, and two different guards stood at the doors to the ICU wing where Steve's room was located. Again they seemed to know Payne on sight. Jay wondered how many times he had been here to see Steve, and why he would have felt it necessary to be there at all. As he had that morning, he could have checked on Steve's condition by phone. Whatever Steve had gotten himself into must be extremely important, and Payne wanted to be on hand the instant he recovered consciousness, if ever.

Payne left her to enter the room on her own, saying he wanted to talk to someone. Jay nodded absently, her attention already focused on Steve. She pushed open the door and walked in, leaving Payne standing in the hall practically in midsentence. A wry, faintly regretful smile touched his mouth as he looked at the closed door; then he turned and walked briskly down the hall.

Jay stared at the man in the bed. Steve. Now that she was seeing him again, it was a little hard to accept that he *was* Steve. She had known Steve as vibrant, burning with energy; he was so still now that it threw her off balance.

He was still in the same position he'd been in the night before; the machines were still quietly humming and beeping, and fluids were still being fed into his veins through needles. The strong scent of hospital antiseptic burned her nose, and suddenly she wondered if, in some corner of his mind, he was aware of the smell. Could he hear people talking, though he was unable to respond?

She walked to the bed and touched his arm as she had the night before. The heat of his skin tingled against her fingertips despite the coolness of the controlled temperature. The mummylike expanse of bandages robbed him of individuality, and his lips were so swollen they looked more like caricatures than the lips of the man she had once kissed, loved, married, fought with and finally divorced. Only the hot bare skin of his arm made him real to her.

Did he feel anything? Was he aware of her touch?

"Steve?" she whispered, her voice trembling. It felt so funny to talk to a motionless mummy, knowing that he was probably so deep in his coma that he was unaware of everything, and that even if by some miracle he could hear her, he wouldn't be able to respond. But even knowing all that, something inside compelled her to try. "I . . . it's Jay." Sometimes he'd called her Jaybird, and when he'd really wanted to aggravate her he'd called her Janet Jean. Her nickname had evolved when she'd been a very young child. Her parents had called her Janet Jean, but her elder brother, Wilson, had shortened it to J.J., which had naturally become Jay. By the time she'd started school, her name was, irrevocably, Jay.

"You've been hurt," she told Steve, still stroking his arm. "But you're going to be all right. Your legs have been broken, and they're both in casts. That's why you can't move them. They have a tube in your throat, helping you to breathe, and that's why you can't talk. You can't see because you have bandages over your eyes. Don't worry about anything. They're taking good care of you here."

Was it a lie that he was going to be all right? Yet she didn't know what else to tell him. If he could hear her, she had to reassure him, not give him something else to worry about.

Clearing her throat, she began telling him about the past five years, what she'd been doing since the divorce. She even told him about being fired, and how badly she'd wanted to punch Farrell Wordlaw right in the nose. How badly she still wanted to punch him in the nose.

The voice was calm and infinitely tender. He didn't understand the words, because unconsciousness still wrapped his mind in layers of blackness, but he heard the voice, felt it, like something warm touching his skin. It made him feel less alone, that tiny, dim contact.

Something hard and vital in him focused on the contact, yearning toward it, forcing him upward out of the blackness, even though he sensed the fanged monsters that waited for him, waiting to tear at his flesh with hot knives and brutal teeth. He would have to endure that before he could reach the voice, and he was very weak. He might not make it. Yet the voice reached out to him, pulling at him like a magnet, lifting him out of the deep senselessness that had held him.

"I remember the doll I got for Christmas when I was four years old," Jay said, talking automatically now. Her voice was low and dreamy. "She was soft and floppy, like a real baby, and she had curly brown hair and big brown eyes, with inch-long lashes that closed when I laid her down. I named her Chrissy, for my very best friend in the world. I lugged that doll around until she was so ragged she looked like a miniature bag lady. I slept with her, I put her on the chair beside me when I ate, and I rode miles around and around the house on my tricycle with her on the seat in front of me. Then I began to grow up, and I lost interest in Chrissy. I put her on the shelf with my other dolls and forgot about her. But the first time I saw you, Steve, I thought, 'He's got Chrissy eyes.' That's what I used to call brown eyes when I was little and didn't know my colors: You have Chrissy eyes."

His breathing seemed to be slower, deeper. She couldn't be certain, but she thought there was a different rhythm to the rise and fall of his chest. The sound of his breathing whistled in and out through the tube in his throat. Her fingers gently rubbed his arm, maintaining the small contact even though something inside her actually hurt from touching his skin.

"I almost told you a couple of times that you have Chrissy eyes, but I didn't think you'd like it." She laughed, the sound warm in the room filled with impersonal, humming machines. "You were always so protective of your macho image. A devil-may-care adventurer shouldn't have Chrissy eyes, should he?"

Suddenly his arm twitched, and the movement so startled her that she jerked her hand away, her face pale. Except for breathing, it was the first time he'd moved, even though she knew it was probably an involuntary muscle spasm. Her eyes flew to his face but there was nothing to see there. Bandages covered the upper two-thirds of his head, and his bruised lips were immobile. Slowly she reached out and touched his arm again, but he lay still under her touch, and after a moment she resumed talking to him, rambling on as she dragged up childhood memories.

Frank Payne silently opened the door and stopped in his tracks, listening to her low murmurings. She still stood by the bed; hell, she probably hadn't moved an inch from the man's side, and she had been in here—he checked his watch—almost three hours. If she had been the guy's wife, he could have understood it, but she was his *ex*-wife, and she was the one who had ended the marriage. Yet there she stood, her attention locked on him as if she were *willing* him to get better.

"How about some coffee?" he asked softly, not wanting to startle her, but her head jerked around anyway, her eyes wide.

Then she smiled. "That sounds good." She walked away from the bed, then stopped and looked back, a frown knitting her brows together. "I hate to leave him alone. If he understands anything at all, it must be awful to just lie there, trapped and hurting and not knowing why, thinking he's all alone.''

"He doesn't know anything," Payne assured her, wishing it was different. "He's in a coma, and right now it's better that he stays in it."

"Yes," Jay agreed, knowing he was right. If Steve were conscious now, he would be in terrible pain.

That first faint glimmer of awareness had faded; the warm voice had gone away and left him without direction. Without that to guide him, he sank back into the blackness, into nothingness.

Frank lingered over the bad cafeteria food and the surprisingly good coffee. It wasn't great coffee; it truly wasn't even good coffee, but it was better than he'd expected. The next batch might not be as good, so he wanted to enjoy this one as long as he could. Not only that, he didn't know exactly how to bring up the subject he'd been skating around all during lunch, but he had to do it. The Man had made it plain: Jay Granger had to stay. He didn't want her to identify the patient and leave; he wanted her to become emotionally involved, at least enough to stay. And what the Man wanted, he got.

Frank had sighed. "What if she falls in love with him? Hell, you know what he's like. He has women crawling all over him. They can't resist him."

"She may be hurt," the Man had conceded, though the steel never left his voice. "But his life is on the line, and our options are limited. For whatever reason, Steve Crossfield was there when it went down. We know it, and they know it. We don't have a list of possibilities to choose from. Crossfield is the *only* choice."

He hadn't needed to say more. Since Crossfield was the only choice, his ex-wife was also the only choice by reason of being the only person who could identify him.

"Did McCoy buy it?" the Man had asked abruptly.

"The whole nine yards." Then Frank's voice had sharpened. "You don't think Gilbert McCoy is—"

The Man interrupted. "No. I know he isn't. But McCoy's a damned sharp agent. If he bought it, that means we're doing a good job of making things look the way we want."

"What happens if she's with him when he wakes up?"

"It doesn't matter. The doctors say he'll be too confused and disoriented to make sense. They're monitoring him, and they'll let us know when they start bringing him out of it. We can't keep her out of his room without it looking suspicious, but watch it. If he starts making sense, get her out of the room fast, until we can talk to him. But there's not too much danger of that happening."

"You're stirring that coffee to death." Jay's voice broke in on his thoughts, and he looked up at her, then down at the coffee. He'd been stirring it so long that it had cooled. He grimaced at the waste of not-bad coffee.

"I've been trying to think of how to ask something of you," he admitted.

Jay gave him a puzzled look. "There's only one way. Just ask."

"All right." He took a deep breath. "Don't go back to New York tomorrow. Will you stay here with Steve? He needs you. He's going to need you even more."

The words hit her hard. Steve had never needed her. She had been too intense, wanting more from him, from their relationship, than he had in him to give. He'd always wanted a slight distance between them, mentally and emotionally, claiming that she "smothered" him. She remembered the time he'd shouted those words at her; then she thought of the man lying so still in the hospital bed, and again she felt that unnerving sense of unreality.

Slowly she shook her head. "Steve is a loner. You should know that from the information you have on him. He doesn't need me now, won't need me when he wakes up, and probably won't like the idea of anyone taking care of him, least of all his ex-wife."

"He'll be very confused when he wakes up. You'll be a lifeline to him, the only face he knows, someone he can trust, someone who'll reassure him. He's in a drug-induced coma...the doctors can tell you more about it than I can. But they've said he'll be very confused and agitated, maybe even delirious. It'll help if someone he knows is there."

Practicality made her shake her head again. "I'm sorry, Mr. Payne. I don't think he'd want me there, but I wouldn't stay anyway, if I could. I was fired from my job yesterday. I have two weeks' notice to work out. I can't afford not to work those two weeks, and I have to find another job."

He whistled through his teeth. "You had a bitch of a day, didn't you?"

She had to laugh, in spite of the seriousness of the situation. "That's a good description of it, yes." The longer she knew Frank Payne, the more she liked him. There was nothing outstanding about him: he was of medium height, medium weight, with graying brown hair and clear gray eyes. His face was pleasant, but not memorable. Yet there was a steadiness in him that she sensed and trusted.

He looked thoughtful. "It's possible we can do something about your situation. Let me check into it before you book a flight back. Would you like a chance to tell your boss to go take a flying leap?"

Jay gave him a very sweet smile, and this time he was the one who laughed.

It wasn't until later that she realized the request meant they were certain Steve would live. She was back in Steve's room, standing by his bed, and she gently squeezed his arm as relief filled her. "You're going to make it," she whispered. It was almost sundown, and she had spent most of the day standing beside his bed. Several times a nurse or an orderly had requested that she step outside, but except for that and the time she had spent with Frank at lunch, she had been with Steve. She had talked until her throat was dry, talked until she couldn't think of anything else to say and silence had fallen again, but even then she had kept her hand on his arm. Maybe he knew she was there.

A nurse came in and gave Jay a curious look but didn't ask her to leave the room. Instead she checked the monitors and made notes on a pad. "It's odd," she murmured. "But maybe not. Somehow I think our boy knows when you're here. His heartbeat is stronger and his respiration rate settles down if you're here with him. When you left for lunch his vital signs deteriorated, then picked back up when you returned. I've noticed the same thing happen every time we've asked you to leave the room. Major Lunning is going to be interested in these charts."

Jay stared at the nurse, then at Steve. "He *knows* I'm here?"

"Not consciously," the nurse said hastily. "He isn't going to wake up and talk to you, not with the barbiturate dose he's getting. But who knows what he senses? You've been talking to him all day, haven't you? Part of it must be getting through, on some level. You must be really important to him, for him to respond to you like this."

The nurse left the room. Stunned, Jay looked back at Steve. Even if he somehow sensed her presence, why would it affect him like that? Yet she couldn't ignore the nurse's theory, because she had noticed herself that the rhythm of his breathing had changed. It was almost impossible for her to believe, because Steve had never needed her in any way. He had enjoyed her for a time, but something in him had kept her at a small but significant distance. Because he couldn't return love of any depth, he hadn't allowed himself to accept a deep love. All Steve had ever wanted was a superficial sort of relationship, a light, playful love that could end with no regrets. Theirs had ended in just that way, and she had seldom thought of him after they had parted. Why should she be important to him now?

Then she gave a low laugh as understanding came to her. Steve wasn't responding to *her*; he was responding to a touch and a voice meant for him personally, rather than the impartial, automatic touches and words of the healers surrounding him. Anyone else would have done just as well. Frank Payne could have stood there and talked to him with the same result.

She said as much an hour later, when Major Lunning studied the charts and stroked his jaw, occasionally glancing at her with a thoughtful expression. Frank stood to one side, careful to keep his face blank, but his sharp gaze didn't miss anything.

Major Lunning was one of the top military doctors, a man devoted to both healing and the military. He wasn't stationed at Bethesda, but he hadn't questioned the orders that had gotten him up in the middle of the night and brought him there. He and several other doctors had been given the task of saving this man's life. At the time they hadn't even known his name. Now there was a name on his chart, but they still had no inkling why he was so important to the powers that be. It didn't make any difference; Major Lunning would use whatever weapon or procedure he could find to help his patient. Right now, one of those weapons was this too-thin young woman with dark blue eyes and a full, passionate-looking mouth.

"I don't think we can ignore the pattern, Ms. Granger," the Major said frankly. "It's your voice he responds to, not mine, not Mr. Payne's, not any of the nurses'. Mr. Crossfield isn't in a deep coma. He's breathing on his own and still has reflexes. It isn't unreasonable to think that he can hear you. He may not understand and he certainly can't respond, but it's entirely possible that he hears."

"But I understood that his coma is drug-induced," Jay protested. "When people are drugged, aren't they totally unconscious?"

"There are different levels of consciousness. Let me explain his injuries more completely. He has simple fractures of both legs, nothing that will prevent him from walking normally. He has second-degree burns on his hands and arms, but the worst of the burns are on his palms and fingers, as if he grabbed a hot pipe, or perhaps put his hands up to shield his face. His spleen was ruptured, and we removed it. One lung was punctured and collapsed. But the worst of his injuries were to his head and face. His skull was fractured, and his facial bones were simply shattered.

"We performed surgery immediately to repair the damage, but to control the swelling of the brain and prevent further damage, we have to administer large doses of barbiturates. That keeps him in a coma. Now, the deeper the coma, the less the brain functions. In a deep coma the patient may not even be able to breathe for himself. The level of the coma depends in part on the patient's tolerance for the drugs, which varies from person to person. Mr. Crossfield's tolerance seems to be a bit higher than usual, so his coma isn't as deep as it could be. We haven't increased the dosage, because it hasn't been necessary. In time we'll gradually decrease the dosage and bring him out of the coma. He's going to make it on his own, but I'll tell you frankly, he definitely does better when you're with him. There's still a lot we don't know about the mind and how it affects the body, but we know it does."

"Are you saying he'll get well faster if I'm here?"

The Major grinned. "That's it in a nutshell."

Jay felt tired and confused, as if she'd spent hours in a house of mirrors trying to find her way out but instead finding only one deceitful reflection after another. It wasn't just these people, all insisting that she stay; part of it was inside. Something happened when she touched Steve, something she didn't understand. She certainly hadn't felt it before, even when they'd been married. It was as if he were more than he had been, somehow different in ways she sensed but couldn't define.

She wished they hadn't put this responsibility on her. She didn't want to stay. This strange feeling she had for Steve made her feel threatened. If she left now, it

wouldn't have a chance to develop. But if she stayed...
She hadn't been devastated by their divorce, five years
earlier, because their love had never grown, never gone
any deeper. In the end it had simply faded away. But
Steve was different now; he'd changed in those five
years, into a man whose power she could feel even when
he was unconscious. If she fell in love with him again,
she might never get over it.

But if she left, she would feel guilty because she
hadn't helped him.

She needed to find another job. She had to get back
to New York and begin doing something to keep her life
from disintegrating. But she was tired of the frantic
pushing and maneuvering, the constant dealing. She
didn't want to go, but she was afraid to stay.

Frank saw the tension in her face, felt it vibrating
through her. "Let's walk down to the lounge," he said,
stepping forward to take her arm. "You need a break.
See you later, Major."

Major Lunning nodded. "Try to talk her into staying. This guy really needs her."

Out in the hall, Jay murmured, "I hate it when people talk around me, as if I'm not there. I'm tired of
being maneuvered." She was thinking of her job when
she said that, but Frank gave her a sharp look.

"I don't mean to put you in a difficult position," he
said diplomatically. "It's just that we badly need to talk
to your husband...sorry, ex-husband. I keep forgetting. At any rate, we're willing to do whatever is possible to aid in his recovery."

Jay put her hands in her pockets, slowing her steps as
she considered something. "Is Steve going to be ar-
rested because of what he was doing, whatever it was?"

Frank didn't have any hesitation on that score. "No," he said with absolute certainty. The man was going to get nothing but the best medicine and best protection his country could provide him; Frank only wished he could tell Jay why, but that wasn't possible. "We think he was simply in the wrong place at the wrong time, an innocent bystander, if you will. But given his background, we think it likely he would have picked up on the situation. It's even possible he was trying to help when everything blew up in his face."

"Literally."

"Yes, unfortunately. Anything he can remember will help us."

They reached the lounge and he opened the door so she could precede him. They were alone, thank heavens. He went over to the coffee machine and fed coins into it. "Coffee?"

"No, thank you," Jay replied tiredly as she sat down. Her stomach was blessedly calm, and she didn't want to upset it now with the noxious brew that usually came from those machines. She hadn't noticed before how tired she was, but now fatigue was washing over her in great waves that made her feel giddy.

Frank sat down opposite her, cradling the Styrofoam cup in his hands. "I talked to my superior, explained your situation," he began. "Would you stay if you didn't have to worry about finding another job?"

She let her eyelids droop as she rubbed her forehead in an effort to force herself to concentrate on what he'd said. She couldn't remember ever having been as tired as she was now, as if all energy had drained from her. Even her mind felt numb. All day long she had focused so fiercely on Steve that everything else had blurred, and now that she had let herself relax, exhaustion had crashed in on her, a deep lassitude that was mental as well as physical.

"I don't understand," she murmured. "I have to work at a job to make money. And even if you've somehow lined one up for me, I can't work and stay here, too."

"Staying here would be your job," Frank explained, wishing he didn't have to push her. She looked as if it were all she could do to sit erect. But maybe she would be more easily convinced now, with fatigue dulling her mind. "We'll take care of your apartment and living expenses. It's that important to us."

Her eyelids lifted and she stared at him incredulously. "You'd *pay* me to stay here?"

"Yes."

"But I don't want money to stay with him! I *want* to help him, don't you understand that?"

"But you can't, because of your financial position," Frank said, nodding. "What we're offering to do is take care of that for you. If you were independently wealthy, would you hesitate to stay?"

"Of course not! I'll do whatever I can to help him, but the idea of taking money for it is ugly."

"We aren't paying you to stay with him, we're paying you so you *can* stay with him. Do you see the difference?"

She had to be going mad, because she did see the difference between the two halves of the hair he had just split. And his eyes were so kind that she instinctively trusted him, even though she sensed a lot going on that she didn't understand.

"We'll get an apartment for you close by, so you can spend more time with him," Frank continued, his voice soothing and reasonable. "We'll also keep your New

York apartment for you, so you'll have that to go back
to. If you give me the word now, we can have a place
here ready for you to move into on Monday.''

There had to be arguments she could use, but she
couldn't think of any. Frank was sweeping all obstacles
out of the way; it would make her feel mean and petty
if she refused to do what he wanted, when he had gone
to so much trouble and they—whoever *they* were—so
badly wanted her to remain.

"I'll have to go home," she said helplessly. "To New
York, that is. I need more clothes, and I'll have to quit
my job." Suddenly she laughed. "If it's possible to quit
a job you've already been fired from."

"I'll make the travel arrangements for you."

"How long do you think I'll be here?" She was estimating a two- or three-week stay, but she wanted to be
certain. She would have to do something about her mail
and utilities.

Frank's gaze was level. "A couple of months, at
least. Maybe longer."

"Months!"

"He'll have to have therapy."

"But he'll be conscious then. I thought you only
wanted me to stay until the worst was over!"

He cleared his throat. "We'd like you to stay until
he's dismissed from the hospital, at least." He had been
trying to break the idea to her gradually, first by just
getting her here, then convincing her that Steve needed
her, then talking her into staying for the duration. He
only hoped it would work.

"But why?"

"He'll need you. He'll be in pain. I haven't told you
before, but he needs more surgery on his eyes. It will
probably be six to eight weeks before he'll get the ban-

dages off his eyes for good. He's going to be confused, in pain, and they'll put him through more pain in therapy. To top it all off, he won't be able to see. Jay, you're going to be his lifeline."

She sat there numbly, staring at him. It looked as if, after all this time and now that it was too late, Steve was going to need her more than either of them had ever thought.

Chapter Three

It felt strange to be back in New York. Jay had flown back on Sunday afternoon and had spent the hours packing her clothes and other personal possessions, but even her apartment had felt strange, as if she no longer belonged there. She packed automatically, her mind on the hospital room in Bethesda. How was he doing? She had spent the morning with him, constantly talking and stroking his arm, yet she felt frantic at spending such a long time away from him.

On Monday morning she dressed for work for the last time, and was conscious of a deep sense of relief. Until it had been lifted, she hadn't been aware what a burden that job had been, how desperately she had been driving herself to compete. Competition was a fine thing, but not at the expense of her health, though part of it could be blamed on her own intensity. She had channeled all her temper, interests and energy into that job, leaving nothing as an escape valve. She was lucky she hadn't developed an ulcer, rather than the less severe stress symptoms of a nervous stomach, constant head-aches and disturbed sleep.

When she reached her office in the high-rise office building that housed many such firms, she scrounged around until she located a cardboard box, then swiftly cleaned out her desk, depositing all her personal items in the carton. There weren't many: a tube of lipstick, an extra pair of panty hose, a small pack of tissues, an expensive gold ballpoint pen, two small prints from the wall. She had just finished and was reaching for the phone to call Farrell Wordlaw to request a meeting when the intercom buzzed.

"Mr. Clements with EchoSystems on line three, Ms. Granger."

Jay depressed the button. "Please transfer all my calls to Duncan Wordlaw."

"Yes, Ms. Granger."

Taking a deep breath, Jay dialed Farrell on the inter-office line. Two minutes later she walked purposefully into his office.

He smiled benignly at her, as if he hadn't cut her off at the knees three days before. "You're looking well, Jay," he said smoothly. "Is something on your mind?"

"Not much," she replied. "I just wanted to let you know that I won't be able to work out the two weeks' notice you gave me. I came in this morning to clean out my desk, and I left instructions for all my calls to be transferred to Duncan."

It gave her a measure of satisfaction to see him blanch. "That's very unprofessional!" he snapped, surging to his feet. "We were counting on you to tie up the loose ends—"

"And train Duncan how to do my job," she interrupted, her voice ironic.

His tone was threatening. "Under these circumstances, I don't see how I can give you the positive recommendation I had planned. You won't work again in investment banking, not without a favorable reference."

Her dark blue eyes were steady and cold as she stared at him. "I don't plan to work in investment banking, thank you."

From that he decided she must already have another job, which took away the leverage he had been planning to use on her. Jay watched him, practically seeing the wheels turning as he considered his options. She was really leaving them in the lurch, and it was his fault, because he had fired her. "Well, perhaps I was too hasty," he said, forcing his voice to show warm paternalism. "It will certainly leave a black eye on this firm, and on you, if the matters on your desk aren't handled properly. Perhaps if I add two weeks' salary as severance pay, you'll reconsider leaving us so precipitately?"

She was supposed to fall back in line when he waved the magic carrot of money in front of her nose. "Thank you, but no," she declined. "It isn't possible. I won't be in town."

Panic began to edge into his face. If the deals she had been handling fell through, it would cost the firm millions of dollars in fees. "But you can't do that! Where will you be?"

Already Jay could imagine panicky phone calls from Duncan. She gave Farrell a cool smile. "Bethesda Naval Hospital, but I won't be accepting any calls."

He looked absolutely stunned. "The...the naval hospital?" he croaked.

"It's a family emergency," she explained as she walked out the door.

When she was outside again with the small cardboard box tucked under her arm, she laughed out loud from the sheer joy of being unemployed, of being able to put that look of panic in Farrell Wordlaw's eyes. It was almost as good as if she had been able to strangle him. And now she was free to return to Steve, drawn by the powerful compulsion to be with him that she could neither understand nor resist.

She had come up on a commuter flight, but because of the amount of luggage and personal furnishings she was taking back to D.C., Frank had arranged for her to take a charter flight back, and she was pleasantly surprised when he met her at the airport. "I didn't know you were going to be here!" she exclaimed.

He couldn't help smiling at her. Her eyes were sparkling like the ocean, and the lines of tension were gone from her face. She looked as if she had thoroughly enjoyed walking out of her job, and he said as much.

"It was...satisfying," she admitted, smiling at him. "How is Steve today?"

Frank shrugged. "Not as well as he was before you left." It was damned strange, but it was true. His pulse was weaker and faster, his breathing shallow and ragged. Even though he was unconscious, the man needed Jay.

Her eyes darkened with worry and she bit her lip. The urge to get back to Steve grew more intense, like invisible chains pulling at her.

But first she had to get settled in the apartment Frank had gotten for her, something that took up too much time and ate at her patience. The apartment was about half the size of her place in New York, really only two rooms—the living room and bedroom. The kitchen was a cubbyhole in a corner, and there was a crowded little alcove for dining. But the apartment was comfortable, especially since she planned to spend most of her time at the hospital, anyway. This was simply a place to sleep and have a few meals.

"I've arranged for you to have a car," Frank said as he carried in the last case. He grinned at her surprised look. "This isn't New York. You'll need a way to get around." He produced the keys from his pocket and dropped them on the table. "You can come and go at the hospital as you like. You have clearance to see Steve at any hour. I won't be around all the time, the way I have been, but whenever I'm gone another agent will be on hand."

"Are you going to the hospital with me now?"

"Now?" he asked, looking surprised in turn. "Aren't you going to unpack?"

"I can unpack later tonight. I'd rather see Steve now."

"All right." Privately he thought the plan was working a little too well, but that couldn't be helped. "Why don't you follow me in your car, so you can get used to the streets and learn the way to the hospital? Uh...you do drive, don't you?"

Smiling, she nodded. "I've only lived in New York for the past five years. Everywhere else I've lived, I needed a car. But I warn you, I haven't driven very much in that time, so give me a chance to get used to it again."

Actually, driving a car was a lot like riding a bicycle: once you had learned, the skill wasn't forgotten. After taking a moment to familiarize herself with the instrumentation, Jay followed Frank's car without difficulty. She had always been a steady, deliberate driver; Steve had been the daredevil, driving too fast, taking chances.

It wasn't until she stepped into his hospital room and approached the bed that she felt a knot of tension deep inside begin to loosen. She stared down at his bandaged head, with only his bruised, swollen lips and jaw visible, and her heart slammed painfully against her ribs. With infinite care she laid her fingers on his arm and began talking.

"I'm here. I had to go back to New York yesterday to pack my things and quit my job. Remind me to tell you about that someday. Anyway, I'm going to be staying here with you until you're better."

The voice was back. Slowly it penetrated the black layers that shrouded his mind, forming a tiny link with his consciousness. He still didn't understand the words, but he wasn't aware that he didn't understand. The voice simply was, like light where before there had been nothing. Sometimes the voice was calm and sometimes it rippled with amusement. He wasn't aware of the amusement, only of the change in tone.

He wanted more. He needed to get closer to the sound, and he began trying to fight his way out of the dark fog in his mind. But every time he tried, a vicious, burning pain that permeated his entire body began gnawing at him, and he would withdraw, back into the protecting blackness. Then the voice would lure him out again, until the beast attacked once more and he had to retreat.

* * *

His arm twitched the way it had once before, and again the movement startled Jay into jerking her hand away. She stopped talking and stared at him. Then, with only a slight pause, she replaced her hand on his arm and resumed what she had been saying. Her heart was pounding. It had to be an involuntary twitching of muscles forced into one position for too long. He couldn't be trying to respond, because the barbiturates they were feeding him literally shut down most of his brain functions. Most, but not all, Major Lunning had said. If Steve was aware of her, could he be trying to communicate?

"Are you awake?" she asked softly. "Can you twitch your arm again?"

His arm was motionless under her fingers, and with a sigh she again took up her rambling discourse. For a moment the feeling had been so strong that she had been convinced he was awake, despite everything they had told her.

She was back at the hospital the next morning before the sun was little more than a graying of the eastern sky. She hadn't slept well, partly because of the unfamiliar surroundings, but she couldn't place all the blame on being in a strange apartment. She had lain awake in the darkness, her mind churning as she tried to analyze and diminish her absurd conviction that, for a moment, Steve had actually been trying to reach out to her in the only way he could. But, for all her analyzing, logic meant nothing whenever she remembered the feeling that had burned through her.

Stop it! she scoffed at herself as she rode the elevator up to the ICU. Her imagination was running away with her, fueled by her own characteristic tendency to totally immerse herself in her interests. She had never been one of those cool, aloof people who could dole out their emotions in careful measure, though she had nearly wrecked her health by trying to be that way. Because she so badly wanted Steve to recover, she was imagining responses where there were none.

His room was bright with lights, despite the hour, since light or darkness hardly mattered to him in his condition. She supposed the nurses left the lights on for convenience. She closed the door, enclosing them in a private cocoon, then walked to his bed. She touched his arm. "I'm here," she said softly.

He drew a deep breath, his chest shuddering slightly.

It hit her hard, jerking at her like a rope that had suddenly been pulled taut. That deep sense of mutual awareness stretching between them, a communication that went beyond logic, beyond speech, was there again, stronger this time. He knew she was there. Somehow he recognized her. And he was fighting to reach her.

"Can you hear me?" she whispered shakily, her eyes locked on him. "Or do you somehow sense my touch? Is that what it is? Can you feel it when I touch your arm? You must be scared and confused, because you don't know what happened and you're trying to reach out, but you can't seem to make anything work. You're going to be all right, I promise you, but it's going to take time."

The voice. Something in it drew him, despite the pain that waited to claw him whenever he left the darkness. He feared the pain, but he wanted the warmth of the voice more. He wanted to be closer to it . . . to her. At some point too dim for him to remember or even comprehend, he had realized it was a woman's voice. It held

*tenderness and the only hint of security in the black
swirling emptiness of his mind and world. He knew very
little, but he knew that voice; some primal instinct in
him recognized it and yearned for it, giving him the
strength to fight the pain and the darkness. He wanted
her to know he was there.*

His arm twitched, the movement somehow too slow
to be an involuntary spasm of cramped muscles. This
time Jay didn't jerk her hand away. Instead she rubbed
her fingertips over his skin, while her eyes fastened on
his face.

"Steve? Did you mean to jerk your arm? Can you do
it again?"

*Odd. Some of the words made sense. Others made no
sense at all. But she was there, closer, the voice clearer.
He could see only darkness, as if the world had never
been, but she was much nearer now. Pain racked his
body, great waves of it that made sweat bead on his
skin, but he didn't want to let go after getting this far,
didn't want to fall back down into the black void.*

*His arm? Yes. She wanted him to move his arm. He
didn't know if he could. It hurt so damned bad he didn't
know if he could hold on, if he could try anymore.
Would she go away if he didn't move his arm? He
couldn't bear being left alone again, where everything
was so cold and dark and empty, not after getting this
close to her warmth.*

*He tried to scream, and couldn't. The pain was in-
credible, tearing him apart like a wild animal with fangs
and claws, ripping at him.*

He moved his arm.

* * *

The movement was barely there, a twitch so light she would have missed it if her hand hadn't been on his arm. He had broken out in a sweat, his chest and shoulders glistening under the bright fluorescent lights. Her heart was pounding as she leaned closer to him, her gaze riveted on his lips.

"Steve, can you hear me? It's Jay. You can't talk because you have a tube in your throat. But I'm right here. I won't leave you."

Slowly his bruised lips parted, as if he were trying to form words that refused to take shape. Jay hung over him, breathing suspended, her chest aching, as he struggled to force his lips and tongue through the motions of speech. She felt the force of both his desperation and dogged determination as, against all logic, he fought pain and drugs to be able to say one word. It was as if he *couldn't* give up, no matter what it cost him. Something in him wouldn't let him give up.

Again he tried, his swollen, discolored lips moving in agonized deliberation. His tongue moved, doing its part to shape the word that would remain soundless:

"Hurt."

The pain in her chest became acute, and abruptly she gulped in deep breaths of air. She didn't feel the tears sliding down her cheeks. Gently she patted his arm. "I'll be right back. They'll give you something so you won't hurt any longer. I'm only leaving you for a minute, and I promise I'll be back."

She flew to the door and jerked it open, stumbling into the hall. She must have been there a lot longer than it seemed, because the third shift had gone home and the first shift was back on duty. Frank and Major Lunning were standing at the nurses' station, talking in low, urgent voices that didn't carry; both men looked up as she ran toward them, and a sort of disbelieving horror filled Frank's eyes.

"He's awake!" she choked. "He said that he hurts. Please, you have to give him something—"

They bolted past her, practically shoving her to the side. Frank said, "This wasn't supposed to happen," in a voice so hard she wasn't certain it was his.

But it had to be, even though the words didn't make any sense. What wasn't supposed to happen? Steve wasn't supposed to wake up? Had they lied to her? Had they expected him to die after all? No, that couldn't be it, or Frank wouldn't have gone to so much trouble to get her to stay.

Nurses were scurrying into Steve's room, but when Jay tried to enter she was firmly escorted back into the hallway. She stood outside, listening to the muted furor of voices inside, chewing on her bottom lip and wiping the slow-welling tears from her cheeks. She should be in there. Steve needed her.

Inside the room, Frank watched as Major Lunning swiftly checked Steve's vital signs and brain-wave activity. "No doubt about it," the major confirmed absently as he worked. "He's coming out of it."

"He's on barbiturates, for God's sake!" Frank protested. "How can he come out of it until you lessen the dosage?"

"He's fighting it off. He's got one hell of a constitution, and that woman out there in the hall has a strong effect on him. Adrenaline is a powerful stimulant. Enough of it, and people perform superhuman feats of strength and endurance. His blood pressure is up and his cardiac output has increased, all signs of adrenaline stimulation."

"Are you going to increase the dosage?"

"No. The coma was to keep his brain from swelling and causing more damage. I was almost ready to begin bringing him out of it anyway. He's just moved up the timetable a little. We'll have to keep him on drugs for the pain, but he won't be in a coma. He'll be able to wake up."

"Jay thought he said that he hurt. Can he feel pain, as drugged as he is?"

"If he was conscious enough to communicate, he was conscious enough to feel pain."

"Can he understand what we're saying?"

"It's possible. I'd say he definitely hears us. Understanding is something else entirely."

"How long will it be before we can question him?"

Major Lunning gave him a severe look. "Not until the swelling in his face and throat subside enough for me to remove the trach tube. I'd say another week. And don't expect him to be a fount of information. He may never remember what happened to him, and even if he eventually does, it could be months in the future."

"Is there any danger that he might reveal some classified information to Jay?" Frank didn't want to say too much. Major Lunning knew that Steve was a very important patient, but he didn't know any of the details.

"It isn't likely. He'll be too dazed and confused, maybe even delirious, and at any rate, he still isn't able to talk. I promise you, you'll be the first to see him when we take the trach tube out."

Frank stared at the still form on the bed; he had been unconscious for so long, it was hard to accept that he could hear or feel, that he had even made an attempt to communicate. But knowing what he knew about the man, Frank realized he should have been prepared for something like this. The man never gave up, never stopped fighting, even when the odds were so strong against him that anyone else would have walked away, and because of that he had survived in many instances when others wouldn't, just as he had this time. Most people never saw past the easy grin to that enormous, fearsome determination.

"What's the likelihood of permanent brain damage?" he asked quietly, remembering that Steve could hear, and there was no way of telling how much he could understand.

Major Lunning sighed. "I don't know. He received excellent, immediate care, and that counts for a lot. It may be so minimal that you won't be able to tell the difference, but I wouldn't put my money on anything right now. I simply can't tell. The fact that he woke up and responded to Ms. Granger is totally out of the expected range. He leapfrogged over several stages of recovery. I've never seen anything like it before. Normally the stages are stupor, where it would take vigorous stimulation to rouse him at all, then delirium and extreme agitation, as if the electrical processes of his brain had gone wild. Then he would become quieter, but he'd be very confused. In the next stage he would be like an automaton. He'd be able to answer questions, but unable to perform any but the simplest physical tasks. The higher brain functions return gradually."

"And the stage he's at now?"

"He was able to communicate, as if he were in the automaton stage, but I think he's lapsed back now. It must have taken a tremendous effort for him to do that much."

"As you cut down on the barbiturates, he'll be able to communicate more?"

"Perhaps. This one incident may not be repeated. He may revert to the more classical stages of recovery."

Exasperated, Frank said, "Is there *anything* you're certain of?"

Major Lunning gave him a long, level look. "Yes. I'm certain that his recovery depends on Ms. Granger. Keep her around. He'll need her."

"Is it safe for her to be with him while you bring him off the drugs?"

"I insist on it. She may keep him calm. I sure as hell don't want him thrashing around with that tube in his chest. Will she be able to take it?"

Frank lifted his brows. "She's stronger than she looks." And Jay was oddly devoted to Steve in a way that he hadn't expected and could not quite under-stand. It was as if something pulled her to him, but there wasn't any basis for that kind of attraction. Maybe later, when he was awake—his effect on women had always had his superiors shaking their heads in disbelief. But he was little more than a mummy now, unable to use the charm for which he was famous, so it had to be something else.

He had to let the Man know what had happened.

Suddenly the door was shoved open and Jay en-tered, giving them a hard, bright look that dared them to throw her out again. "I'm staying," she said flatly, moving to Steve's side and putting her hand on his arm. Her chin lifted stubbornly. "He needs me, and I'm going to be here."

Major Lunning looked from her to Steve, then at Frank. "She's staying," he said mildly, then consulted the file in his hand. "Okay, I'm going to begin decreas-ing the barbiturates now, to completely bring him out of the coma. It will take from twenty-four to thirty-six hours, and I don't know how he's going to react, so I want him under full-time observation." He glanced up at Jay. "Ms. Granger—may I call you Jay?"

"Please," she murmured.

"A nurse will be in here with him most of the time until he's completely off the drugs. His reaction may be unpredictable. If anything happens, it's important that you move away from the bed and not hinder anything we have to do. Do you understand?"

"Yes."

"Can I trust you not to faint and get in the way?"

"Yes."

"All right. I'll hold you to that." His stern military gaze measured her, and he must have been reassured by what he saw, because he gave an abrupt nod of approval. "It won't be easy, but I think you'll hold up."

Jay turned her attention back to Steve, dismissing everyone else in the room as if they no longer existed. She couldn't help it. He crowded everyone else out of her consciousness, flattening them into one-dimensional cartoon characters. Nothing mattered except him, and since his agonized attempt to talk to her, the feeling was even stronger than before. It shattered her and terrified her, because it was so far outside her previous experience, but she couldn't fight it. It was so strange; Steve was exerting far more power over her now than he ever had before, when he'd had full use of his senses and body, and his full range of charm. He was motionless and, for the most part, insensate, but something deep and primal pulled her to him. Just being in the same room with him made her heart settle into a stronger rhythm, heating her flesh as her blood raced through her veins, energizing her.

"I'm back," she murmured, touching his arm. "You can go to sleep now. Don't worry, don't fight the pain... just let it go. I'm here with you, and I won't leave. I'll watch over you, and I'll be here when you wake up again."

Slowly his breathing settled into an easier rhythm and his pulse rate dropped. His blood pressure lowered. Air hissed from the tube in his throat in what would have been a faint sigh had the tube not been in place. Jay stood by his bed, her fingers lightly stroking his arm as he slept.

Where are you? He came awake, screaming silently as he clawed his way through the shrouding darkness and pain into an even greater horror. The pain was like being eaten alive, but he could bear that because despite its force, it was secondary to the horrible emptiness. God, was he buried alive? He couldn't move, couldn't see, couldn't make a sound, as if his body had died but his mind had remained alive. Terrified, he tried again to scream and couldn't.

Where was he? What had happened?

He didn't know. God help him, he didn't know!

"I'm here," the voice crooned soothingly. "I know you're frightened and don't understand, but I'm here. I'll stay with you."

The voice. It was familiar. It had been in his dreams. No, not dreams. Something deeper than that. It was in his guts, his bones, his cells, his genes, his chromosomes. It was part of him, and he focused on it with an intense, almost painful recognition. Yet it was oddly alien, connected to nothing his conscious mind could produce.

"The doctors say you're probably very confused," the voice continued. It was a calm, tender voice, with a slightly husky catch in it, as if she had been crying. She. Yes. It was definitely a woman. He had a vague memory of that voice calling to him, pulling him out of a strange, suffocating darkness.

She began reciting a litany of injuries, and he listened to her voice with fierce concentration, only gradually realizing that she was talking about him. He was injured. Not dead, not buried alive.

The tidal wave of relief exhausted him.

She was still there the next time he surfaced, and this time the initial terror was of shorter duration. Fractionally more alert, he decided she was hoarse rather than teary.

She was always there. He had no concept of time, only of pain and darkness, but gradually he became aware that there were two darknesses. One was in his mind, paralyzing his thoughts, but he could fight it. Slowly that darkness was becoming less. Then there was the other darkness, the absence of light, the inability to see. Again he would have panicked if she hadn't been there. Over and over she explained, as if she knew he would only gradually comprehend her words. He wasn't blind; there were bandages over his eyes, but he wasn't blind. His legs were broken, but he would walk again. His hands were burned, but he would use them again. There was a tube in his throat to help him breathe; soon the tube would be removed and he would talk again.

He believed her. He didn't know her, but he trusted her.

He tried to think, but words boomeranged around in his head until he couldn't make sense of them. He didn't know... There was so much he didn't know. He didn't know anything. But he couldn't catch the words and arrange them in proper order so he'd know what it was he didn't know. It just didn't make sense, and he was too tired to fight.

Finally he woke to find that his thoughts were clearer, the confusion different, because the words made sense even though nothing else did. She was there. He could feel her hand on his arm, could hear her slightly hoarse voice. Did she stay with him all the time? How long had it been? It seemed forever, and it nagged at him, because he felt as if he should know exactly.

There was so much he wanted to know, and he couldn't ask. Frustration ate at him, and his arm flexed beneath her fingers. God, what would happen to him if she left? She was the one link he had to the world outside the prison of his own body, his link to sanity, the only window in his world of darkness. And suddenly the need to know coalesced inside him into a single thought, a single word: *Who?*

His lips formed the word and gave birth to it in silence. Yes, that was the word he'd wanted. Everything he wanted to know was summed up in that one small word.

Jay gently laid her fingers over his swollen lips. "Don't try to talk," she whispered. "Let's use a spelling system. I'll recite the alphabet, and whenever I get to the letter you want, twitch your arm. I'll do the alphabet over and over until we've spelled out whatever you want to say. Can you do that? One twitch for yes, two twitches for no."

She was exhausted; it had been two days since the first time he had woken up, and she had been with him for most of that time. She had talked until her voice was almost gone, her words giving him a bridge out of his coma into reality. She knew when he was awake, sensed that he was terrified, felt his struggle to understand what had happened. But this was the first time his lips had moved, and she was so tired she hadn't been able to grasp what he'd been trying to say. The alphabet game was the only way she could think of for them to communicate, but she didn't know if he'd be able to concentrate enough for it to work.

His arm twitched. Just once.

She drew a deep breath, forcing her exhaustion away. "All right. Here we go. A...B...C...D..."

She began to give up hope as she slowly ran through the alphabet and his arm lay motionless under her hand. It had been a long shot, anyway. Major Lunning had said it could be days before Steve's mind would be clear enough for him to really understand what was going on around him. Then she said "W," and his arm twitched.

She stopped. "W?"

His arm twitched. Once, for "Yes."

Joy shot through her. "Okay, W is the first letter. Let's go for the second one. A...B..."

His arm twitched on the H.

And again on the O.

He stopped there.

Jay was astounded. "*Who?* Is that it? You want to know who I am?"

His arm twitched. *Yes.*

He didn't know; he really didn't know. She couldn't remember if she had mentioned who she was, except when she had first begun talking to him. Had she thought he would remember her voice after not seeing her for five years?

"I'm Jay," she said gently. "Your ex-wife."

Chapter Four

He was very still. Jay had the impression that she could feel him withdrawing, though he didn't move a muscle. A surprisingly sharp pain bloomed inside, and she chided herself for it. What had she expected? He couldn't get up and hug her, he couldn't speak, and he was probably exhausted. She knew all that, yet she still had the feeling that he was pulling back from her. Did he resent being so dependent on her? Steve had always been aloof in a curious sort of way, holding people away from him. Or maybe he resented the fact that she was here with him now, rather than some impersonal nurse. After all, a certain degree of independence remained when the service was detached, done because it was a job. Personal service carried a price that couldn't be paid in dollars, and Steve wouldn't like that.

She schooled her voice to a calmness she didn't feel. "Do you have any more questions?"

Two twitches. *No.*

She had been pushed away so many times that she recognized it now, even as subtle and unspoken as the message was. It hurt. She closed her eyes, fighting for the control that would let her speak again. It was a moment before she managed it. "Do you want me to stay in here with you?"

He was still for a long moment. Then his arm twitched. And twitched again. *No.*

"All right. I won't bother you again." Her control was shot, her voice thin and taut. She didn't wait to see if he made any response, but turned and walked out. She felt almost sick. Even now, it was an effort to walk out and leave him alone. She wanted to stay with him, protect him, fight for him. God, she would even take his pain on herself if she could. But he didn't want her. He didn't need her. She had been right all along in thinking that he wouldn't appreciate her efforts on his behalf, but the pull she thought she had felt between them had been so strong that she had ignored her own good sense and let Frank talk her into staying.

Well, at least she should let Frank know that her sojourn here was over, and that she would be leaving. Her problems hadn't changed; she still had to find a new job. Digging a coin out of her purse, she found a pay phone and called the number Frank had given her. He hadn't spent as much time at the hospital these past two days as he had before; in fact, he hadn't been there at all that day.

He answered promptly, and hearing his calm voice helped. "This is Jay. I wanted you to know that my job is over. Steve doesn't want me to stay with him anymore."

"What?" He sounded startled. "How do you know?"

"He told me."

"How in blue blazes did he do that? He can't talk, and he can't write. Major Lunning said he should still be pretty confused, anyway."

"He's a lot better this morning. We worked out a system," she explained tiredly. "I recite the alphabet, and he signals with his arm when I get to the letter he wants. He can spell out words and answer questions. One twitch means 'Yes' and two twitches means 'No.'"

"Have you told Major Lunning?" Frank asked sharply.

"No, I haven't seen him. I just wanted to let you know that Steve doesn't want me with him."

"Have Lunning paged. I want to talk to him. Now."

For such a pleasant man, Frank could be commanding when he chose, Jay thought as she went to the nurses' station and requested that Major Lunning be paged. It was five minutes before he appeared, looking tired and rumpled, and dressed in surgicals. He listened to Jay, then, without a word, walked to the pay phone and talked quietly to Frank. She couldn't make out what he was saying, but when he hung up he called a nurse and went directly into Steve's room.

Jay waited in the hallway, struggling to handle her feelings. Though she knew Steve and had expected this, it still hurt. It hurt more now than it had when they had divorced. She felt oddly...betrayed, and bereft, as if she had lost part of herself, and she hadn't felt that way before. She hadn't felt so strongly connected to him before. Well, this was just another classic example of her own intensity leading her to read things into a situation that simply weren't there. Would she ever learn?

Major Lunning was in Steve's room a long time, and a phalanx of nurses came and went. Within half an hour Frank arrived, his face taut and set. He squeezed Jay's arm comfortingly as he went past, but he didn't stop to talk. He, too, disappeared into Steve's room, as if something dreadfully important were going on in there.

Jay moved to the visitors' lounge, sitting quietly with her hands folded in her lap while she tried to plan what she should do next. Return to New York, obviously, and get a job. But the idea of hurling herself back into the business world left her cold. She didn't want to go back. She didn't want to leave Steve. Even now, she didn't want to leave him.

Almost an hour later Frank found her in the lounge. He looked at her sharply before going to the coffee machine and buying two cups. Jay looked up and managed a smile for him as he approached. "Do I really look as if I need that?" she asked wryly, nodding toward the coffee.

He extended a cup toward her. "I know. It tastes worse than it looks. Drink it anyway. If you don't need it now, you will in a minute."

She took the cup and sipped the hot liquid, grimacing at the taste. It was a mystery how anyone could take simple water and coffee and make them taste so horrible. "Why will I need it in a minute? It's over, isn't it? Steve told me to go away. It's obvious that he doesn't want me here, so my presence will only upset him and slow his recovery."

"It isn't over," Frank said, looking down at his own coffee, and his flat tone made Jay look at him sharply. He looked haggard, with worry etching new lines into his face.

A cold chill ran down her spine and she sat up straight. "What's wrong?" she asked. "Has he relapsed?"

"No."

"Then what's wrong?"

"He doesn't remember," Frank said simply. "Anything. He has amnesia."

Frank had been right; she did need the coffee. She drank that cup, then got another one. Her head was reeling, and she felt as if she'd been punched in the stomach. "What else can go wrong?" she asked, talking mostly to herself, but Frank knew what she meant.

He sighed. They hadn't counted on this. They had needed him awake, able to talk, able to understand what needed to be done. This latest development had thrown a monkey wrench into the whole plan. He didn't even know who he was! How could he protect himself if he didn't know who he had to be on guard against? He couldn't recognize friends or enemies.

"He's been asking for you," Frank said, taking her hand. She started, already rising to her feet, but he tugged on her hand and she sank back into her chair. "We've been asking him a lot of questions," he continued. "We used your system, though it takes a while. When you told him you were his ex-wife, it confused him, scared him. He couldn't remember you, and he didn't know what to do. Remember, he's still easily confused. It's hard for him to concentrate, though he's getting better fast."

"Are you certain he's asking for me?" Jay asked, her heart pounding. Out of everything he had said, her emotions had centered on his first sentence.

"Yes. He spelled out your name over and over."

The instinct to go to him was so strong it was almost painful. She forced herself to sit still, to understand more. "He has total amnesia? He doesn't remember anything?"

"He doesn't even know his own name." Frank sighed again, a heavy sound. "He doesn't remember anything about the explosion or why he was there. Nothing. A total blank. Damn it!" The last expressed his helpless frustration.

"What does Major Lunning think?"

"He said total amnesia is extremely rare. More often it's a sort of spot amnesia that blocks out the accident itself and anything that happened a short while before it. With the head trauma Steve suffered, amnesia wasn't that unexpected, but this..." He made a helpless gesture.

She tried to think of what she had read about amnesia, but all that came to mind was the dramatic use often made of it on soap operas. Invariably the amnesiac recovered his full memory during a highly dramatic moment, just in time to prevent a murder or keep from being murdered himself. It was good melodrama, but that was all it was.

"Will he regain his memory?"

"Probably. Part of it, at least. There's no way to be certain. It might start coming back almost immediately, or it could take months before he begins remembering anything. Major Lunning said that his memory will come back in bits and pieces, usually the oldest memories first."

Might. Probably. Could. Usually. What it all added up to was that they simply didn't know. In the meantime Steve lay in his bed, unable to talk, unable to see, unable to move. All he could do was hear and think.

What would it be like to be so cut adrift from everything familiar, even himself? He had no point of reference for anything. The thought of the inner terror he must be feeling squeezed her heart.

"Are you still willing to stay?" Frank asked, his clear eyes filled with concern. "Knowing that it might take months or even years?"

"Years?" she echoed faintly. "But you only wanted me to stay until the surgery on his eyes was completed."

"We didn't know then that he wouldn't remember anything. Major Lunning said that being around familiar things and people would help stimulate his memory, give him a feeling of stability."

"You want me to stay until he regains his memory," Jay stated, putting it into words. The idea frightened her. The longer she stayed with Steve, the more strongly she reacted to him. What would happen to her if she fell in love with him far more deeply than she had the first time, only to lose him again when he returned to his footloose life? She was afraid that she already cared too much to simply walk away. How could she walk away when he needed her?

"He needs you," Frank said, echoing her thoughts. "He's asking for you. He responds to you so strongly that he keeps confounding Major Lunning's predictions. And we need you, Jay. We need you to help him in any way you can, because we need to know what he knows."

"If sentiment won't get me, try patriotism?" she asked tiredly, leaning her head back against the padded orange vinyl chair. "It wasn't necessary. I won't leave him. I don't know what's going to happen, or how we'll handle it if he doesn't get his memory back soon, but I won't leave him."

She got up and walked out, and Frank sat there for a moment staring at the cup still in his hands. From what she'd just said, he knew that Jay sensed she was being manipulated, but she was willing to let them do it because Steve was so important to her. He had to talk to the Man about this latest development, and he wondered what would happen. They had counted on Steve's willing participation, on his talents and skills. Now they had to let him walk out on the streets as helpless as a baby because he couldn't recognize the dangers, or take the risk of telling him things that could set back his recovery. Major Lunning had been adamant that upsetting him would be the worst thing they could do. He needed quiet and tranquillity, a stable emotional base; his memory would return faster under those conditions. No matter what decision the Man reached, Steve was at risk. And if Steve was at risk, so was Jay.

It was hard for Jay to enter Steve's room after the emotional battering she had taken. She needed time to get herself under control, but she felt the pull between them again; it was growing so strong she no longer had to be in the room with him, touching him. He needed her right now, far more than she needed time. She opened the door and felt his attention center on her, though not even his head moved. It was as if he were holding his breath.

"I'm back," she said quietly, walking to his bed and putting her hand on his arm. "It seems I can't stay away."

His arm twitched urgently, several times, and she got the message. "All right," she said, and began reciting the alphabet.

Sorry.

What could she say? Deny that she'd been upset? He would know better. He felt the pull just as she did, because he was on the other end of that invisible rope. He turned his face slightly toward her, his bruised lips parted as he waited for her answer.

"It's all right," she said. "I didn't realize what a shock I had just given you."

Yes.

It was odd how much expression he could put in a single motion, but she felt his wryness and sensed that he was still shocked. Shocked, but in control. His control was astounding.

She began spelling again.

Afraid.

The admission hit her hard; it was something the old Steve never would have admitted, but the man he had become was so much stronger that he could admit it and lose nothing of his strength. "I know, but I'll stay with you as long as you want me," she promised.

What happened? He made it a question by a slight upward movement of his arm.

Keeping her voice calm, Jay told him about the explosion but didn't give him any of the details. Let him think that he'd simply been in an accident.

Eyes?

So he hadn't understood everything she'd told him before and needed reassuring. "You'll have more surgery on your eyes, but the prognosis is good. You'll see again, I promise."

Paralyzed?

"No! You've broken both legs and they're in casts. That's why you can't move them."

Toes.

"Your toes?" she asked in bewilderment. "They're still there."

His lips moved in a very slight, painful smile. *Touch them.*

She bit her lip. "Okay." He wanted her to touch his toes so he'd know he still had feeling in them, as a reassurance that he wasn't paralyzed. She walked to the foot of the bed and firmly folded her hands over his bare toes, letting his cool flesh absorb the heat from her palms. Then she returned to his side and touched his arm. "Did you feel that?"

Yes. Again he gave that painful fraction of a smile.

"Anything else?"

Hands.

"They're burned, and in bandages, but they're not third-degree burns. Your hands will be fine."

Chest. Hurts.

"You have a collapsed lung, and a tube in your chest. Don't do any tossing around."

Funny.

She laughed. "I didn't know anyone could be silent and sarcastic at the same time."

Throat.

"You have a trach tube because you weren't breathing well."

Face broken?

She sighed. He wanted to know, not be protected. "Yes, some bones in your face were broken. You aren't disfigured, but the swelling made it hard for you to breathe. As soon as the swelling goes down, they'll take the trach tube out."

Lift the sheet and check my—

"I will not!" she said indignantly, halting her spelling when she realized where his words were heading. Then she had to laugh because he actually managed to look impatient. "Everything is still there, believe me."

Functional?

"You'll have to find that out on your own!"

Prissy.

"I'm not prissy, and you behave or I'll have a nurse change your tube. Then you'll find out the hard way what you want to know." As soon as she said the words she felt herself blushing, and it didn't help that he was smiling again. She hadn't meant to sound the way she had.

The effort of concentrating for so long had tired him, and after a minute he spelled *Sleep.*

"I didn't mean to tire you out," she murmured. "Go to sleep."

Stay?

"Yes, I'm staying. I won't go back to my apartment without telling you." Her throat felt thick at his need for reassurance, and she stood by the bed with her hand on his arm until his breathing changed into the deep, steady rhythm of sleep.

Even then she was reluctant to take her hand away, and she stood beside him for a long time. A smile kept curving her lips. His personality was so strong that it came through despite his limited means of communication. He wanted the truth about his condition, not vague promises or medical double-talk. He might not know his name, but that hadn't changed the man he was. He was strong, much stronger than he had been before. Whatever had happened to him in the past five years had tempered him, like steel subjected to the hottest fires. He was harder, stronger, tougher, his willpower so fierce it was like an energy field emanating from him. Oh, he had been a charming rascal before, devilishly reckless and daring, with a glint in his eye that had turned many feminine heads. But now he was...dangerous.

The word startled her, but when she examined it, she realized that it described exactly the man he had become. He was a dangerous man. She didn't feel threatened by him, but danger didn't necessarily constitute a threat. He was dangerous because of his steely, implacable will; when this man decided to do something, it wasn't safe to get in his way. At some time in the past five years, something had drastically changed him and she wasn't sure she wanted to know what it was. It must have been something cataclysmic, something awful, to have so focused his character and determination. It was as if he had been stripped down to the bare essentials of human existence, forced to discard all his personality traits that weren't necessary to survival and adopt new ones that were. What was left was hard and pure, unbreakable and curiously resilient. This was a man who wouldn't admit defeat; he didn't know what it was.

Her heart was beating heavily as she stood looking down at him, her attention so focused on him that they might have been the only two people in the world. He awed her, and he attracted her so strongly that she jerked her hand away from his arm as soon as the thought formed. Dear God! She would be a fool to let herself get caught in that trap again. Even more now than before, Steve was essentially alone, his personality so honed that he was complete unto himself. She had walked away relatively unscathed before, but what would happen to her this time if she let herself care too much? She felt scared, not only because she was teetering on the edge of heartbreak, but because she was even daring to think of getting too close to him. It was like watching a panther in a cage, standing outside the bars and knowing you were safe, but feeling the danger that was barely restrained.

Making love with him before had been ... fun, passionate in a playful way. What would it be like now? Was the playfulness gone? She thought it must be. His lovemaking would be intense and elemental now, as he was, like getting caught up in a storm.

She became aware that she could barely breathe, and she forced herself to walk away from his bed. She didn't want him to mean that much to her. And she was very much afraid that he already did.

"What do we do?" Frank asked quietly, his clear eyes meeting shuttered black ones.

"We play out the hand," the Man answered just as quietly. "We have to. If we do anything out of the ordinary now, it could tip someone off, and he isn't able to recognize his enemies."

"Any luck in tracing Piggot?"

"We lost him in Beirut, but we know he hooked up with his old pals. He'll surface again, and we'll be waiting."

"We just have to keep our guy alive until we can neutralize Piggot," Frank said, his tone turning glum.

"We'll do it. One way or the other, we have to keep Piggot's cutthroats from getting their hands on him."

"When he gets his memory back, he isn't going to like what we've done."

A brief smile touched the Man's hard mouth. "He'll raise mortal hell, won't he? But I'm not taking any chance with the protected-witness program until he's able to look out for himself, and maybe not even then. It's been penetrated before, and could be again. Everything hinges on getting Piggot."

"You ever wish you were back in the field, so you could hunt him yourself?"

The Man leaned back, hooking his hands behind his head. "No. I've gotten domesticated. I like going home at night to Rachel and the kids. I like not having to watch my back."

Frank nodded, thinking of the time when the Man's back had been a target for every hit man and terrorist in the business. He was safe now, out of the mainstream . . . as far as was generally known. A very small group of people knew otherwise. The Man officially didn't exist; even the people who followed his orders didn't know the orders came from him. He was buried so deeply in the bowels of bureaucracy, protected by so many twists and turns, that there was no way to connect him to the job he actually did. The President knew about him, but Frank doubted the vice president did, or any department secretary, the Chiefs of Staff or the head of the agency that employed him. Whoever was President next might not know about him. The Man decided for himself whom he could trust; Frank was one of those people. And so was the man in Bethesda Naval Hospital.

Two days later, they took the tube out of Steve's chest because his collapsed lung had healed and reinflated. When they let Jay into his room again she hung over the side of his bed, stroking his arm and shoulder until his breathing settled down and the fine mist of perspiration on his body began to dry.

"It's over, it's over," she murmured.

He moved his arm, a signal that he wanted to spell, and she began reciting the alphabet.

Not fun.

"No," she agreed.

More tubes?

"There's one in your stomach, for feeding you." She felt his muscles tense as if in anticipation of the pain he knew would come, and he spelled out a terse expletive. Her hand moved over his chest in sympathy, feeling the coarseness of his hair as it grew out, and avoiding the wound where the tube had entered his body.

He took a deep breath and forced himself to slowly relax. *Raise head.*

It took her a few seconds to figure that one out. He must be incredibly sore from lying flat for so long, unable to shift his legs or lift his arms. The only time his arms were moved was when the bandages were changed. She pressed the control that raised the head of the bed, lifting him only an inch or so at a time, keeping her hand on his arm so he could signal her when he wanted her to stop. He took several more deep breaths as his weight shifted to his hips and lower back, then moved his arm to halt her. His lips moved in silent curse, his muscles tightening against the pain, but after a moment he adjusted and began to relax again.

Jay watched him, her deep blue eyes mirroring the pain he felt, but he was improving daily, and seeing the improvements filled her with heady joy. The swelling in his face was subsiding; his lips were almost normal again, though dark bruises still stained his jaw and throat.

She could almost feel his impatience. He wanted to talk, he wanted to see, he wanted to walk, to be able to shift his own weight in the bed. He was imprisoned in his body and he didn't like it. She thought it must be close to hell to be cut off from his own identity as he was, as well as being so completely constrained by his injuries. But he wasn't giving in; he asked more questions every day, trying to fill the void of memories by making new ones, maybe hoping that some magic word would take him back to himself. Jay talked to him even when he didn't ask questions, idle conversation that, she hoped, gave him basic information and perspective. Even if it just filled the silence, that was something. If he didn't want her to talk he would tell her.

A movement of his arm alerted her, and she began the alphabet.

When married?

She caught her breath. It was the first personal question he'd asked her, the first time he'd wanted to know about their past relationship. "We were married for three years," she managed to say calmly. "We divorced five years ago."

Why?

"It wasn't a hostile divorce," she mused. "Or a hostile marriage. I guess we simply wanted different things out of life. We grew apart, and finally the divorce seemed more like a formality than any wrenching change in our lives."

What did you want?

Now that was a twenty-thousand-dollar question. What did she want? She had been certain of her life up until the Friday when she had been fired and Frank Payne had brought Steve back into her life. Now she wasn't certain at all; too many changes had happened all at once, jolting her life onto a different track entirely. She looked at Steve and felt him waiting patiently for her answer.

"Stability, I guess. I wanted to settle down more than you did. We had fun together, but we weren't really suited to each other."

Children?

The thought startled her. Oddly, when they had been married, she hadn't been in any hurry to start a family. "No, no children." She hadn't been able to visualize having Steve's children. Now... oh God, now the idea shook her to the bones.

Remarried?

"No, I've never remarried. I don't think you have, either. When Frank notified me of your accident, he asked if you had any other relatives or close friends, so you must have stayed single."

He'd been listening closely, but his interest suddenly sharpened. She could feel it, like a touch against her skin. *No family?*

"No. Your parents are dead, and if you had any relatives, I never knew about them." She skated around telling him that he'd been orphaned at an early age and raised in foster homes. Not having a family seemed to disturb him, though he'd never given any indication that it bothered him while they had been married.

He lay very still and the line of his mouth was grim. She sensed there was a lot he wanted to ask her, but the very complexity of his questions stymied him. To get his mind off the questions he couldn't ask and the answers he wouldn't like, she began to tell him about how they had met, and slowly his mouth relaxed.

"...and since it was our first date, I was a little stiff. More than a little stiff, if you want the truth. First dates are torment, aren't they? It had been raining off and on all day, and water was standing in the streets. We walked out to your car, and a passing truck hit this huge puddle just as we reached the curb. We were both drenched, from the head down. And we stood there laughing at each other like complete fools. I don't even want to think what I looked like, but you had muddy water dripping off your nose.''

His lips were twitching, as if it hurt him to smile but he couldn't stop the movement. *What did we do?*

She chuckled. ''There wasn't a lot we could do, looking the way we did. We went back to my apartment, and while our clothes were washing we watched television and talked. We never did make it to the party we'd been going to. One date led to another, and five months later we were married.''

He asked one question after another, like a child listening to fairy tales and wanting more. Knowing that he was reaching for the part of himself that was lost due to the blankness of his memory, she tirelessly recounted places they had gone and the things they'd done, people they had known, hoping that some little detail would provide the spark needed to bring it all back. Her voice began to grow hoarse, and finally he managed a small shake of his head.

Sorry.

She pressed his arms, understanding. ''Don't worry,'' she said softly. ''It will all come back. It will just take time.''

But the days passed and still his memory didn't return—not even a glimmer of a link to the past. She could feel his intense concentration on every word she uttered, as if he were willing himself to remember. Even now, his control was phenomenal; he never allowed himself to become frustrated or lose his temper. He just kept trying, keeping his feelings under control as if he sensed that any emotional upheaval could set his recovery back. Total recovery was his aim, and he worked toward it with a single-minded concentration that never wavered.

Frank was there the day they took the trach tube from Steve's throat, and he waited in the hall with Jay, holding her hand. She looked at him questioningly, but he merely shook his head. Several minutes later a hoarse cry of pain from Steve's room made her jerk, and Frank's hand tightened on hers. "You can't go in there," he said softly. "They're removing his stomach tube, too."

The cry had been Steve's; the first sound he'd made had been one of pain. She began to tremble, every instinct she had screaming at her to go to him, but Frank held her still. There were no other sounds from the room, and finally the door opened and the doctors and nurses exited. Major Lunning was last, and he paused to talk to Jay.

"He's all right," he said, smiling a little at her tense face. "He's breathing just fine, and talking. I won't tell you what his first words were. But I want to warn you that his speaking voice won't be the way you remember it; his larynx was damaged, and his voice will always sound hoarse. It will improve some, but he'll never sound the way he did before."

"I'd like to talk to him now," Frank said, looking down at Jay, and she understood that there were things he wanted to tell Steve, even though Steve didn't remember what had happened.

"Good luck," Major Lunning said, smiling wryly at Frank. "He doesn't want you, he wants Jay, and he was pretty autocratic about it."

Knowing just how autocratic he could be, Frank wasn't surprised. But he still needed to ask Steve some questions, and if this was his lucky day, the questions just might trigger some return of memory. Patting Jay's hand again, he went into Steve's room and firmly closed the door behind him.

Less than a minute later, he opened the door and looked at Jay, his expression both frustrated and amused. "He wants you, and he isn't cooperating until he gets you."

"Did you think I would?" a raspy voice demanded behind him. "Jay, come here."

She began trembling again at the sound of that rough, deep voice, so much rougher and deeper than she remembered. It was almost gravelly, and it was wonderful. Her knees felt rubbery as she crossed the room to him, but she wasn't aware of actually walking. She was just there, somehow, clinging to the railing of his bed in an effort to hold herself upright. "I'm here," she whispered.

He was silent a moment; then he said, "I want a drink of water."

She almost laughed aloud, because it was such a mundane request that could have been made of anyone, but then she saw the tension in his jaw and lips and realized that, again, he was checking out his condition, and he wanted her with him. She turned to the small Styrofoam pitcher that was kept full of crushed ice, which she used to keep his lips moist. The ice had melted enough that she was able to pour the glass half full of water. She stuck a straw into it and held it to his lips.

Gingerly he sucked the liquid into his mouth and held it for a moment, as if letting it soak into his membranes. Then, slowly, he swallowed, and after a minute he relaxed. "Thank God," he muttered hoarsely. "My throat still feels swollen. I wasn't sure I could swallow, and I sure as hell didn't want that damned tube back."

Behind Jay, Frank turned a smothered laugh into a cough.

"Anything else?" she asked.

"Yes. Kiss me."

Chapter Five

When she opened the door to Steve's room the next morning, he turned his head on the pillow and said, "Jay." His voice was harsh, almost guttural, and she wondered if he'd just awakened.

She paused, her attention caught as she stared at his bandaged eyes. "How did you know?" The nurses were in and out, so how could he have guessed her identity?

"I don't know," he said slowly. "Maybe your smell, or just the feel of you in the room. Maybe I recognize the rhythm of your walk."

"My smell?" she asked blankly. "I'm not using perfume, so if you smell me from that distance something's wrong!"

His lips curved in a smile. "It's a fresh, faintly sweet smell. I like it. Do I get a good-morning kiss?"

Her heart gave a giant leap, just as it had the day before when he'd demanded that she kiss him. She had given him a light, tender kiss, barely brushing her lips against his, while Frank, in the background, had pretended to be invisible; but it had taken her pulse a good ten minutes to settle down afterward. Now, even while her mind shouted at her to be cautious, she crossed the room to him and bent down to give him another light kiss, letting her lips linger for only a second. But when she started to draw away, he increased the pressure, his mouth molding itself to hers, and her heart slammed wildly against her rib cage as excitement shot through her.

"You taste like coffee," she managed to say when she finally forced herself to stand upright again, breaking the contact.

His lips had been slightly parted, with a disturbing sensuality, but at her words they took on a smug line. "They wanted me to drink tea or apple juice—" he made it sound like hemlock "—but I talked them into letting me have coffee."

"Oh?" she asked dryly. "How? By refusing to drink anything until you had your coffee?"

"It worked," he said, not sounding at all repentant. She could imagine how helpless the nurses were against his relentless will.

Despite the fact that she no longer needed to communicate with him in their old way, her hand went to his arm in habit, and she was so used to the contact that she didn't notice it. "How are you feeling?" she asked, then winced at the triteness of the question, but she was still rattled from the effects of his kiss.

"Like hell."

"Oh."

"How long have I been here?"

To her surprise, she had to stop and count the days. She had become so involved with him that time had ceased to mean anything, and it was difficult to recall. "Three weeks."

"Then I have three more weeks in these casts?"

"I think so, yes."

"All right." He said it as if giving his permission, and she felt that he would give them three weeks and not one day longer, or he would take the casts off himself. He lifted his left arm. "I'm minus a couple of needles today. They took the IVs out about an hour ago."

"I hadn't even noticed!" she exclaimed, smiling a little at the note of pride in his ruined voice. She wondered if she would ever get used to its harshness, but at the same time tiny shivers went down her spine every time she heard it.

"And I refused the pain medication. I want my head clear. There were a lot of questions I wanted to ask before, but it took so much time and effort, and my brain was so foggy from the drugs, that it was just too much trouble. Now I want to know what's going on. Where am I? I've heard you call the doctor Major, so I know I'm in a military hospital. The question is, why?"

"You're in Bethesda," she said.

"A naval hospital?" Astonishment roughened his voice even more.

"Frank said you were brought here for security reasons. There are guards posted at every entrance to this wing. And this was a central location for all the surgeons they pulled in for you."

"Major Lunning isn't navy," he said sharply.

"No." It was astonishing that he could lose the most basic of memories, those of himself, yet retain the knowledge that Bethesda was a naval hospital and that major wasn't a navy rank. She watched the stillness of his mouth as he studied the implications of what she had just told him.

"Then someone with a lot of influence wanted me here. Langley, probably."

"Who?"

"Company headquarters, baby. CIA." She felt a chill of dread as he continued, "Maybe the White House, but Langley is the most likely bet. What about Frank Payne?"

"He's FBI. I trust him," she said steadily.

"Damn, this is getting deep," he muttered. "All these different departments and military branches coordinating just isn't normal. What's going on? Tell me about the explosion."

"Didn't Frank tell you?"

"I didn't ask for or volunteer any information. I didn't know him."

Yes, that was like Steve. He had always held back, watching cautiously, though she had already married him before she began noticing that particular trait. He used his charm like a shield, so that most people would have described him as outgoing and spontaneous, when in fact he was just the opposite. He had held people away, not trusting them and not allowing anyone close to him, but they never noticed, because he was such an actor. Now she sensed that the shield was gone. People could take him as he was or leave him; he didn't care. It was a hard attitude, but she found that she liked it better. It was real, without pretense or subterfuge. And for the first time, he was letting her get close to him. He needed her, trusted her. Perhaps it was only because of the extenuating circumstances, but it was happening, and it stunned her.

"Jay?" he prompted.

"I don't know exactly what happened," she explained. "I don't know why you were there. They don't know either."

"Who is 'they'?"

"Frank. The FBI."

"And whoever else he's working for," he added dryly. "Go on."

"Frank told me that you weren't doing anything illegal that they know of. Perhaps you were only an innocent bystander, but you have a reputation for sniffing out trouble, and they think you might know something about what happened to their operation. They had set up a sting, or whatever you want to call it, but someone had planted a bomb at the meeting site. You were the only survivor."

"What kind of sting?"

"I don't know. All Frank has said is that it involved national security."

"And they're afraid their guy's cover was blown, but they don't know, because the players on the other side were disintegrated, too," he said, as if to himself. "It could have been a double double-cross, and the bomb was meant for the others. Damn! No wonder they want me to get my memory back! But all that doesn't explain one thing. Why are you involved?"

"They brought me here to identify you," she said, absently stroking his arm as she had for so many hours.

"Identify me? Didn't they know?"

"Not for certain. Part of your driver's license was found, but they still weren't certain if you were . . . you, or their agent. Apparently you and the agent were about the same height and weight, and your hands were burned, so they weren't able to get your fingerprints for identification.'' She paused as something nagged at her memory, but she couldn't bring the elusive detail into focus. For a moment it was close; then Steve's next question splintered her concentration.

''Why did they ask you? Wasn't there anyone else who could identify me? Or did we stay close after our divorce?''

''No, we didn't. It was the first time I'd seen you in five years. You've always been pretty much a loner. You weren't the type for bosom buddies. And you don't have any family, so that left me.''

He moved restlessly, his mouth drawing into a hard line as he uttered a brief, explicit curse. ''I'm trying to get a handle on this,'' he said tersely. ''And I keep running into this damned blank wall. Some of what you tell me seems so familiar, and I think, yeah, that's me. Then part of it is as if you're telling me about some stranger, and I wonder if I really know. Hell, how *can* I know?'' he finished with raw frustration.

Her fingers glided over his arm, giving him what comfort she could. She didn't waste her breath mouthing platitudes because she sensed they would only make him furious. As it was, he had already used up his small store of energy with the questions he had asked her, and he lay there in silence for several minutes, his chest rising and falling too quickly. Finally the rhythm of his breathing slowed, and he muttered, ''I'm tired.''

''You've pushed yourself too far. It's only been three weeks, you know.''

''Jay.''

''What?''

''Stay with me.''

''I will. You know I will.''

"It's...strange. I can't even picture your face in my mind, but part of me knows you. Maybe biblical knowledge goes deeper than mere memory."

His harsh voice gave rough edges to the words, but Jay felt as if an electrical charge had hit her body, making her skin tingle. Her mind filled with images, but not those of memory; her imagination manufactured new ones—of this man with his harder soul and ruined voice, bending over her, taking her in his arms, moving between her legs in a more complete possession than she had ever known before. Her own breath shortened as her breasts grew tight and achy, and her insides turned liquid. Another tingle jolted her, making her feel as if she were on the verge of physical ecstasy, and merely from his words, his voice. The violence of her response shocked her, scared her, and she jerked away from his bed before she could control the motion.

"Jay?" He was concerned, even a little alarmed, as he felt her move away from him.

"Go to sleep," she managed to say, her voice almost under control. "You need the rest. I'll be here when you wake up."

He lifted his bandaged hand. "How about holding my hand?"

"I can't do that. It would hurt you."

"It would blend in with all the other pain," he said groggily. He was losing strength rapidly. "Just touch me until I go to sleep, all right?"

Jay felt his request go straight through her heart. That he should ask anything of her still staggered her, but his need to be touched was almost more than she could bear. She stepped back to the bed, folding her hand over his arm. At the first touch she felt him begin to relax, and within two minutes he was asleep.

She stepped outside, feeling the need to escape, though she wasn't certain exactly what she was escaping from. It was Steve, and yet it was something else, something inside her that was growing more and more powerful. It scared her; she didn't want it, yet she was helpless to stop it. She had never responded to him like that before, not even in the first wild, heady days of their marriage. It's just the situation, she told herself, trying to find comfort in the thought. It was just her tendency to throw herself wholly into something, concentrating on it too intensely, that made her feel like this. But comfort eluded her and despair welled in her heart, because analyzing her emotions didn't change them. God help her, she was falling in love with him again, with even less reason than she'd had the first time. For most of the past three weeks he'd been little more than a mummy, incapable of movement or speech, yet she had felt drawn to him, tied to him; and loving him now was much more dangerous than it had been before. He was a different, stronger, harder man. Even when he'd been unconscious, she had felt his fierce inner power, and her need to know what had happened to him to cause that change was so strong it almost hurt.

A nurse, the one who had first noticed Steve's unconscious reaction to Jay's presence, stopped beside her. "How is he? He refused his pain medication this morning."

"He's asleep now. He tires very easily."

The nurse nodded, her bright blue eyes meeting Jay's darker ones. "He has the most incredible constitution I've ever seen. He's still in a great deal of pain, but he just seems to ignore it. Normally it would be at least another week before we began tapering off the pain medication." Admiration filled her voice. "Did the coffee upset his stomach?"

Jay had to laugh. "No. He was rather smug about it."

"He was certainly determined to get that coffee. Maybe we can start him on a soft diet tomorrow, so he can begin regaining his strength."

"Do you know when he'll be transferred out of intensive care?"

"I really don't know. Major Lunning will have to make that decision." The nurse smiled as she took her leave, returning to the central station.

Jay walked to the visitors' lounge to buy a soft drink, and she took advantage of the room's emptiness to give herself some much-needed privacy. She was filled with a vague uneasiness, and she couldn't pinpoint the reason. Or reasons, she thought. Part of it was Steve, of course, and her own unruly emotional response to him. She didn't want to love him again, but she didn't know how to fight it, only that she had to. She *could not* love him again. It was too risky. She knew that, fiercely told herself over and over that she wouldn't allow it to happen, even as she acknowledged that it might already be too late.

The other part of her uneasiness was also tied to Steve, but she wasn't certain why. That aggravating sense of having missed something kept nagging at her, something that she should have seen but hadn't. Perhaps Steve sensed it too, judging by all the questions he'd asked; he didn't quite trust Frank, though she supposed that was to be expected, given Steve's situation. But Jay knew that she would trust Frank with her life, and with Steve's. So why did she keep feeling that she should know more than she did? Was Steve in danger because of what he had witnessed? Had Steve actually been involved in the deal? She would have had to be naive not to realize that the vast majority of the facts had been kept from her, but she didn't expect Frank to spout out everything he knew. No, it wasn't that. It was something that she should have seen, something that was obvious, and she'd missed it entirely. It was some little detail that didn't fit, and until she could pinpoint what it was, she wouldn't be able to get rid of that nagging uneasiness.

Steve was taken out of intensive care two days later and moved to a private room, and the navy guards shifted location. The new room had a television, something the ICU room had lacked, and Steve insisted on listening to every news program he could, as if he were searching for clues that would tie all the missing pieces together for him again. The problem was that he seemed to be interested in all the world situations and could discuss the politics of others nations as easily as domestic issues. That disturbed Jay; Steve had never been particularly political, and the depth of his current knowledge revealed that he had become deeply involved. Given that, it became more likely that he had also been more involved in the situation that had nearly killed him than perhaps even Frank knew. Or perhaps Frank did know, after all. He had had several long, private conversations with Steve, but Steve remained guarded. Only with Jay did he lose his wariness.

His various injuries kept him bed-bound much longer than he should have been, but he wasn't able to negotiate with crutches due to his burned hands. His physical inactivity ate at him, eroding his patience and good humor. He quickly decided which television shows he liked, discarding all game shows and soap operas, but even the ones he liked lacked something, since so much of the action was visual. Merely being able to listen frustrated him, and soon he wanted the set on only for the news. Jay did everything she could think of to entertain him; he liked it when she read the newspaper to him, but for the most part he just wanted to talk.

"Tell me what you look like," he said one morning.

The demand flustered her. It was oddly embarrassing to be asked to describe oneself. "Well, I have brown hair," she began hesitantly.

"What shade of brown? Reddish? Gold?"

"Gold, I guess, but on the dark side. Honey-colored."

"Is it long?"

"No. It's almost to my shoulders, and very straight."

"What color are your eyes?"

"Blue."

"Come on," he chided after a minute when she didn't add anything. "How tall are you?"

"Medium. Five-six."

"How tall am I? Did we fit together well?"

The thought made her throat tighten. "You're six feet, and yes, we did dance well together."

He turned his bandaged eyes toward her. "I wasn't talking about dancing, but so what? When I get out of these casts, let's go dancing again. Maybe I haven't forgotten how."

She didn't know if she could stand being in his arms again, not with her responses running wild every time she heard his harsh, cracked voice. But he was waiting for her to answer, so she said lightly, "It's a date."

He lifted his hands. "The bandages come off tomorrow. Next week I have the final surgery on my eyes. The casts come off in two weeks. Give me a month to build up my strength. By then the bandages should be off my eyes, and we'll do the town.''

''You're only giving yourself a month to get your strength back? Isn't that a little ambitious?''

''I've done it before,'' he said, then went very still. Jay held her breath as she watched him, but after a minute he swore softly. ''Damn it, I *know* things, but I can't remember them. I know what foods I like, I know the name of every head of state of every nation mentioned in the news, I can even recall what they look like, but I don't know my own face. I know who won the last World Series, but not where I was when it was played. I know the smell of the canals in Venice, but I can't remember ever being there.'' He paused a minute, then said very quietly, ''Sometimes I want to take this place apart with my bare hands.''

''Major Lunning told you what to expect,'' Jay said, still shaken by what he'd said. How deeply had he involved himself in the gray world Frank had hinted at? She was very much afraid that Steve was no longer an adventurer, but a player. ''Stop feeling sorry for yourself. He said your memory would probably come back in dribbles.''

A slow grin touched his lips, deepening the lines that bracketed his mouth and drawing her helpless, fascinated gaze. His lips seemed firmer, fuller, as if they were still slightly swollen, or perhaps it was because his face was thinner and older. ''Sorry,'' he said. ''I'll have to watch that.''

His wry humor, especially when he had good reason to occasionally feel sorry for himself, only reminded her again of his hard inner strength and was one more blow against the shaky guard she had set up around her heart. She had to laugh at him, just as she had years before, but there was a difference now. Before, Steve had used humor as a wall to hide behind; now the wall was gone, and she could see the real man.

She was with him the next morning when the bandages came off his burned hands for good. She had been in there before when the bandages were changed, so she had seen the raw blisters on his palms and fingers when they had looked much worse than they did now. Patches of reddened skin were still visible all the way to his elbows, but his hands had caught the worst of it. Now that the danger of infection was past, the new, tender skin would heal faster without the bandages, but his hands would be too painful for him to use them much for a while.

When she compared how he looked now to the way he had looked the first time she had seen him, hooked to all those machines and monitors, with so many tubes running into his body, it seemed nothing short of a miracle. It had been only four weeks, but he had been little more than a vegetable then, and now he exerted the force of his personality over everyone who entered his room, even the doctors. His face had been swollen and bruised before; now the hard line of his jaw and the precise cut of his lips fascinated her. She knew that plastic surgeons had rebuilt his shattered face, and she wondered about the changes she would see when the bandages were completely gone and she was able to truly see him for the first time. His jaw was a little different, a little squarer, leaner, but that was to be expected, since he had lost so much weight after he'd been injured. His beard seemed darker, because he was so pale. She was very well acquainted with his jaw and beard, since she had to shave him every morning. The nurses had done it until he became conscious and made it known he wanted Jay to shave him, and no one else.

He no longer had a thick swath of gauze wrapped around his skull. There was a big, jagged white scar that ran diagonally from the top of his head, at a point directly above his right ear, to the back and left of his skull, but his hair was already longer than that of the average military recruit in boot camp, and it was beginning to cover the scar. The new hair was dark and glossy, having never been exposed to the sun. His eyes were still covered with bandages, but though the gauze pads and wrapping were much smaller now than they had been before, the upper bridge of his nose and the curve of his cheekbones were still covered. The bandages tantalized her; she wanted to see his new face, to judge for herself how well the plastic surgeon had done his job. She wanted to be able to apply his identity to his face, to look into his dark eyes and see all the things she'd looked for in their marriage and hadn't been able to find.

"Your hands are tender," the doctor who'd been caring for Steve's burns said as he cut away the last of the bandages and signaled for a nurse to clean them. "Be careful with them until all this new skin has toughened. They're stiff right now, but use them, exercise them. You don't have any tendon or ligament damage, so in time you'll have full use of them again."

Slowly, painfully, Steve flexed his fingers, wincing as he did so. He waited until the doctor and nurses had left the room, then said, "Jay?"

"I'm here."

"How do they look?"

"Red," she answered honestly.

He flexed them again, then cautiously rubbed the fingers of his right hand over his left one, then reversed the procedure. "It feels strange," he said, smiling a little. "They're damned tender, like he said, but the skin feels as smooth as a baby's butt. I don't have any calluses now." The smile faded abruptly, replaced with a frown. "I had callused hands." Again he explored his hands, as if trying to find something familiar in the touch, slowly rubbing his fingertips together.

She laughed softly. "One summer, you played so much sandlot baseball that your hands were as tough as leather. You had calluses on your calluses."

He still looked thoughtful; then his mood changed and he said, "Come sit by me, on the bed."

Curious, she did as he said, sitting facing him. The head of his bed had been raised to an upright position, so he was sitting erect and they were on the same level. Abruptly she noticed how much she had to look up at him. His bare shoulders and chest, despite the weight he had lost, still dwarfed her, and again she wondered what sort of work he had done that had developed his torso to that degree.

Tentatively he reached out, and his hand touched her hair. Realizing why he had wanted her to sit there, she remained still while his fingers sifted through the strands. He didn't say anything. He lifted his other hand, and his palms cupped her face, his fingers gliding lightly over her forehead and brow, down the bridge of her nose, over her lips and jaw and chin before sliding down the length of her throat.

Her breath had stopped, but she hadn't noticed. Slowly he laced his fingers around her neck as if measuring it, then traced the hollows of her collarbones out to her shoulders. "You're too thin," he murmured, cupping the balls of her shoulders in his palms. "Don't you eat enough?"

"Actually, I've gained a little weight," she whispered, beginning to shake at his warm touch.

Calmly, deliberately, he moved his hands down to her breasts and molded his fingers over them. Jay inhaled sharply, and he said, "Easy, easy," as he stroked the soft mounds.

"Steve, no." But her eyes were closing as warm pleasure built in her, her blood beating slowly and powerfully through her veins. His thumbs rubbed over her nipples and she quivered, her breasts beginning to tighten.

"You're so soft." His voice roughened even more. "God, how I've wanted to touch you. Come here, sweetheart."

He ignored the pain in his hands as he pulled her against him, and he wrapped his arms around her as he had dreamed of doing so many times since her voice had charmed him out of the darkness. He felt her slenderness, her softness, her warmth, and the gut-wrenching pleasure of her breasts flattening against the hard planes of his chest. He smelled the sweetness of her skin, felt the thick silk of her hair, and with a harsh, muffled sound of want, of need, he sought her mouth.

He already knew her mouth. He would beg, cajole, insist until she would give him a kiss in the morning and again at night before she left. He knew it was wide and full and soft, and that her lips trembled each time she kissed him. Now he slanted his mouth to cover hers, pressing hard until her lips parted and gave him the entrance he sought. He could feel her shaking in his arms as he moved his tongue into her mouth and tasted her sweetness. Damn, how had he been fool enough to let her get away from him five years before? Not being able to remember making love to her made him furious because he wanted to know what she liked, how it felt to be inside her, if they had been as good together as every instinct he possessed told them they would be. She belonged to him; he knew it, felt it, as if they were tied together. He deepened the kiss, forcing her to respond to him the way he knew she could, the way he knew she wanted to. Finally she shivered convulsively, and her tongue met his as her arms crept up around his neck.

He shouldn't be this strong, Jay thought dimly, not after all he's been through. But his arms were hard, and so tight around her that her ribs were being squeezed. Steve had never been this aggressive before; he certainly hadn't been a passive man, but now he was kissing her with naked demand, forcing their relationship into an intimacy that frightened her. He wanted her more than he ever had during their marriage, but now his attention was intensely focused on her because of the circumstances.

"We shouldn't do this," she managed to say, turning her head aside to free her mouth from the hungry pressure of his. She brought her hands down and pushed lightly at his shoulders.

"Why not?" he murmured, taking advantage of the vulnerability of her throat with slow kisses. His tongue touched the sensitive hollow below her ear, and her hands tightened on his shoulders as wonderful little ripples of pleasure radiated over her skin. His lack of sight didn't hinder him; he knew his way around a woman's body. Instinct went deeper than memory.

Both conscience and her sense of self-protection made Jay push at his shoulders again, and this time he slowly released her. "We can't let ourselves get involved again," she said in a low voice.

"We're both free," he pointed out.

"As far as we know. Steve, you could have met someone in the past five years who you really care about. Someone could be waiting for you to come home. Until you get your memory back, you can't be certain that you're free. And...and I think we should be cautious about jumping back into a relationship without knowing more than we do."

"No one's waiting for me," he said with harsh certainty.

Her movements were jerky with agitation as she slid off the bed and walked to the window. The morning sky was a leaden color, and snow flurries were drifting aimlessly on the light wind. "You can't know that," she insisted, and turned back to look at him.

His face was turned toward her even though he couldn't see her, and the hard line of his mouth told her he was angry. The sheet was around his waist, baring his broad shoulders and chest, as he had disdained both pajamas and a hospital gown, though he had finally consented to wear the pajama bottoms with the legs cut off and the seams slit so they would fit over the casts on his legs. He was thin, pale and weak from what he'd been through, but somehow the impression he gave was one of power. Nor was he all that weak, not if the strength she had just felt in him was any measure. He must have been incredibly strong before the accident. Those five years when she hadn't seen him were becoming even more of a mystery.

"So you've stayed here with me all this time just because you have a Florence Nightingale complex?" he asked sharply. It was the first time she had refused him anything, and he didn't like it at all. If he could have walked, he would have come after her, sightless or not, weak or not, even though he was still in pain most of the time. None of that would have stopped him, and for the first time she was grateful for his broken legs.

"I never hated you," she tried to explain, knowing that she owed him at least the effort. "I don't think we were all that deeply in love, certainly not enough to make our marriage work. Frank asked me to stay because he thought you would need me, given your condition. Even Major Lunning said it would help if you were around someone familiar, someone you knew before the accident. So . . . I stayed."

"Don't give me that crap." Her attempt to explain had made him even more furious, and it was a type of anger she hadn't seen before. He was very still and controlled, his guttural voice little more than a whisper. Chills ran up her spine because she could feel his temper like both ice and fire, lashing out at her even though he hadn't moved. "Do you think that because I can't see, I couldn't tell you were turned on just now? Try again, sweetheart."

Jay began to get angry at the harsh demand in his voice. "All right, if you want the truth, here it is. I don't trust you. You were always too restless to settle down and try to build a life together. You were always leaving on another of your 'adventures,' looking for something I couldn't give you. Well, I don't want to go through that again. I don't want to get involved with you again. You want me now, and you may need me a little, but what happens when you're well? Another pat on the head and a kiss on the cheek while I get to watch you ride off into the sunset? Thanks, but no thanks. I have more sense now than I did before."

"Is that why you start shaking every time I touch you? You want to get involved again, all right, but you're afraid."

"I said I don't trust you. I didn't say I was afraid of you. Why should I trust you? You were still looking for trouble when that explosion almost killed you!"

Abruptly she realized that she was all but yelling at him, while his voice hadn't risen at all. She turned and walked out, then leaned against the wall outside his door until both the temper and the shaking subsided. She felt sick, not because of their argument, but because he was right. She *was* afraid. She was terrified. And it was too late to do anything about it, because she was in love with him again, despite all her warnings and lectures to herself against it. She didn't know him anymore. He had changed; he was harder, rougher, far more dangerous. He was still a leaver, probably far more involved in the situation than Frank had wanted her to know.

But it didn't make any difference. She had loved him before when it had gone against her better judgement, and she loved him now when it made even less sense. God help her, she had left herself wide open for a lot of pain, and there was nothing she could do.

Chapter Six

Steve lay quietly, forcing the lingering cloudiness of anesthesia from his mind. He was instinctively still, like an animal in the jungle, until he was aware enough to know what was going on. A man could lose his life by moving before he knew where his enemies were. If they thought he was dead, he gained the advantage of surprise by lying still and not letting them know he was still alive until he could recover enough to make his move. He tried to open his eyes, but something covered them. They had him blindfolded. But that didn't make sense; why blindfold someone they thought was dead?

He listened, trying to locate his captors. The usual jungle sounds were absent, and gradually he realized that he was too cold to be in a jungle. The smell was all wrong, too; it was a sharp, medicinal odor, like disinfectant. This place smelled like a hospital.

The realization was like a curtain going up, and abruptly he knew where he was and what had happened, and at the same time the hazy recollection of the steamy jungle swiftly faded. The final surgery on his eyes was over, and he was in Recovery. "Jay!" It took an incredible amount of effort to call for her, and his voice sounded strange, even worse than usual, so deep and hoarse it was almost like an animal's cry. "Jay!"

"Everything's all right, Mr. Crossfield," a calm voice said soothingly. "You've had your surgery, and everything is just fine. Lie still, and we'll have you back in your room in a few minutes."

It wasn't Jay's voice. It was a nice voice, but it wasn't what he wanted. His throat was dry; he swallowed, and winced a little because his throat was so raw and sore. That's right; they'd had a tube down it. "Where's Jay?" he croaked, like a frog.

"Is Jay your wife, Mr. Crossfield?"

"Yes." Ex-wife, if they wanted to get technical. He didn't care about the labels. Jay was his.

"She's probably waiting for you in your room."

"Take me there."

"Let's wait a few more minutes—"

"Now." The single word was guttural, the steely command naked. He didn't try to dress it up in polite phrases, because it was all he could do to say a few words at a time. He was still groggy, but he fixed his thoughts on Jay with single-minded determination. He began groping for the rail on the side of the bed.

"Mr. Crossfield, wait! You're going to pull the IV out of your arm!"

"Good," he muttered.

"Calm down, we're going to take you to your room. Just lie still while I get an orderly."

A minute later he felt the bed begin to move. It was a curiously relaxing movement, and he began to go to sleep again but forced himself to stay alert. He couldn't afford to relax until Jay was with him; there was damned little he knew about who he was or what was going on, but Jay was the one constant in his life, the one person he trusted. She had been there from the beginning, as far back as his memory reached, and further.

"Here we are," the nurse said cheerfully. "He couldn't wait to get back to his room, Mrs. Crossfield. He was asking for you and kicking up a fuss."

"I'm here, Steve," Jay said, and he thought she sounded anxious. He noticed that she didn't correct the nurse about her name, and fierce satisfaction filled him. The name didn't mean much to him, but it was a name he'd once shared with Jay, one of the links that bound her to him.

He was lifted onto his bed, and he could feel them fussing around him for a few more minutes. It was getting harder to stay awake. "Jay!"

"I'm here."

He reached out with his left hand toward her voice, and her slim, cool fingers touched him. Her hand felt so small and fragile in his.

"The doctor said everything went perfectly," she said, her voice somewhere above him in the darkness. "You'll get the bandages off for good in about two weeks."

"Then I'm outta here," he murmured. His hand tightened around hers, and he gave in to the lingering effects of the anesthesia.

When he woke again, it was without the initial confusion, but he was still groggy. Impatiently he forced his

mind out of lethargy, and it was so habitual now to ignore the pain in his mending body that he truthfully
didn't even notice it. At some unknown point in his life
he had learned that the human body could be forced to
superhuman feats if the brain knew how to ignore pain.
Evidently he had learned that lesson so well that it was
second nature to him now.

Now that he was more awake, he didn't have to call
for Jay to know she was in the room. He could hear her
breathing, hear the pages of a magazine turning as she
sat by the bed. He could smell the faint, sweet scent of
her skin, a scent that identified her immediately to him
whenever she entered the room. Then there was that
other awareness, the physical awareness that was like an
electrical charge, making his skin tingle with pleasure
and excitement at her closeness, or even at the mere
thought of her.

He hadn't kissed her since their argument the week
before, but he was only biding his time. She had been
upset, and he didn't want that, didn't want to push her.
Maybe he hadn't been much of a prize before, but she
still felt something for him, or she wouldn't be here
now, and when the time came he would capitalize on
those feelings. She was his; he knew it with a bone-deep
sense of possession that overrode everything else.

He wanted her. The strength of his sexual need for
her surprised him, given his current physical condition, but the stirring in his loins every time she touched
him was proof that certain instincts were stronger than
pain. Every day the pain was a little less, and every day
he wanted her a little more. It was basic. Whenever two
people were attracted to each other, the urge to mate
became overwhelming; it was nature's way of propa-
gating the species. Intense physical desire and hot, fre-

quent lovemaking reinforced the bond between two people. They became a couple, because back in the human species' first primitive days, it took two people to provide care for their helpless young. In current times one parent could raise a child quite well, and modern medicine had made it possible for a woman not to become pregnant if she didn't want to, but the old instincts were still there. The sexual drive was still there, a man's need to make love to his woman and make certain she knew she was his. He understood the basis of the biological need programmed into his genes, but understanding didn't lessen its power.

Amnesia was a curious thing. When he examined it unemotionally, he was interested in its oddities. He had lost all conscious knowledge of whatever had happened to him before he'd come out of the coma, but a lot of unconscious knowledge evidently hadn't been affected. He could remember different World Series and Super Bowls, and how Niagara Falls looked. That wasn't important. Interesting, but not important.

Equally interesting, and far more important, were the things he knew about both obscure Third World nations and major powers without remembering how he came by the knowledge. He couldn't bring his own face to mind, but somehow that didn't negate what he knew was fact. He knew the desert, the hot, dry heat and blood-sizzling sun. He also knew the jungle, the stifling heat and humidity, the insects and reptiles, the leeches, the shrieking birds, the stench of rotting vegetation.

Taking those bits and pieces of himself that he could recognize, he was able to piece together part of the puzzle. The jungle part was easy. Jay had told him that he was thirty-seven; he was just the right age to have been in Vietnam during the height of the war in the late sixties. The rest of it, all added together, could have only one logical explanation: he was far more involved in the situation than Jay had been told.

He had wondered if scopolamine or Pentothal would be successful on an amnesia victim, or if the amnesia effectively sealed off his memories even from the powerful drugs available today. If what he might know was important enough for him to warrant this kind of red-carpet treatment, then it would have been worth Frank Payne's effort to at least have tried the drugs. They hadn't tried, and that told him something else: Payne knew Steve had been indoctrinated to resist any chemical prying into his brain. Therefore he must be a trained field operative.

Jay didn't know. She really thought he had simply been in the wrong place at the wrong time. She had said that when they had been married, he had constantly been taking off on one "adventure" after another, so he must have kept her in the dark and just let her think that he was footloose, rather than worrying her with the knowledge of just how dangerous his work was, and that the odds were even he wouldn't return from any given trip.

He had fitted that many pieces of the puzzle together, but there were still a lot of little things that didn't make sense to him. He had noticed, as soon as the bandages were taken off his hands, that his fingertips were oddly smooth. It wasn't the smoothness of scar tissue; his hands were so sensitive, with their new, healing skin, that he could tell the difference between the burned areas and his fingertips. He was positive his fingertips hadn't been burned; rather, his fingerprints had been altered or removed altogether, probably the latter. Recently, too, most likely here in this hospital. The question was: Why? Who were they hiding his identity from? They knew who he was, and he was evidently on good terms with them, or they wouldn't have gone to such extraordinary lengths to save his life. Jay knew who he was. Was someone out there hunting for him? And, if so, was Jay in danger simply because she was with him?

Too many questions, and he didn't know the answers to any of them. He could ask Payne, but he wasn't certain he'd get a straight answer from the man. Payne was hiding something. Steve didn't know what it was, but he could hear a faint note of guilt in the man's voice, especially when he spoke to Jay. What had they gotten Jay involved in?

He heard the door to his room open and he lay motionless, wanting to know the identity of his visitor without them knowing he was awake. He had noticed that cautiousness in himself before; it fit in with what he had deduced.

"Is he awake yet?"

It was Frank Payne's quiet voice, and that special note was there again, the guilt and the . . . affection. Yeah, that's what it was. Payne liked Jay and worried about her, but he was still using her. It made Steve feel even less inclined to cooperate. It made him mad, to think they could be putting Jay in any danger.

"He went to sleep as soon as they got him in bed, and he hasn't stirred since. Have you talked to the doctor?"

"No, not yet. How did it go?"

"Wonderfully. The doctor doesn't think there's any permanent damage. He has to lie as quietly as possible for a few days, and his eyes may be sensitive to bright light after the bandages come off, but he probably won't even need glasses."

"That's good. He should be leaving here in another couple of weeks, if everything goes all right."

"It's hard to think of not coming here every day," Jay mused. "It won't seem normal. What happens when he's released?"

"I need to talk to him about that," Payne answered. "It can wait a few days, until he's more active."

Steve could hear the worry in Jay's voice and wondered at it. Did she know something, after all? Why else would she worry about what happened to him when he left the hospital? He had news for her, though; wherever she went, that was where he intended to go, and Frank Payne could take those ideas of his and become real friendly with them.

Two more weeks of biding his time. He didn't know if he could do it. It was hard to force himself to exercise the patience he needed to allow his body to heal, and there were still weeks of rehabilitation ahead before he regained his full strength. He'd have to push himself harder than the therapists would, but he could sense his own limits, and he knew they were more elastic than the therapists could guess. It was just one more piece of the puzzle.

He decided to let himself "wake up" and began shifting restlessly. The IV needle tugged at his hand. "Jay?" he called in a groggy tone, then cleared his throat and tried again. "Jay?" He never quite got used to hearing his own voice the way it was now, so harsh and strained, gravelly in texture. Another little oddity. He couldn't remember his own voice, but he knew this one wasn't right.

"I'm here." Her cool fingers touched his arm.

How many times had he heard those two words, and how many times had they provided him with a link to consciousness? They seemed embedded in his mind, as if they were his one memory. Hell, they probably were. He reached for her with his free hand. "Thirsty."

He heard the sound of water pouring; then a straw touched his lips and he gratefully sucked the cold liquid into his dry mouth and down his raw throat. She took the straw away after only a couple of swallows. "Not too much at first," she said in that calm way of hers. "The anesthesia may make you sick."

He moved his hand and felt the needle tugging at it again. Swift irritation filled him. "Get a nurse to take this damned needle out."

"You need glucose after surgery to keep from going into shock," she argued. "And it probably has an antibiotic in it—"

"Then they can give me pills," he rasped. "I don't like being restricted like this." It was bad enough that his legs were still in casts; he'd had enough of having to lie still to last him a lifetime.

She was silent for a moment, and he could sense her understanding. Sometimes it was as if they didn't need words, as if there were a link between them that transcended the verbal. She knew exactly how frustrated it made him to have to lie in bed day after day; it was not only boring, it went against every survival instinct he possessed. "All right," she finally said, her cool fingers drifting against his arm. "I'll get a nurse."

He listened as she left the room, then lay quietly, waiting to see if Frank Payne would identify himself. It was a subtle game; he didn't even know why he was playing it. But Payne was hiding something, and Steve didn't trust him. He'd do anything he could to gain an edge, even if it was something so trivial as pretending to sleep while he eavesdropped. He hadn't even learned anything, other than that Payne had "plans" for him.

"Are you in any pain?" Frank asked.

Steve cautiously turned his head. "Frank?" Another part of the game, pretending he didn't recognize the other man's voice.

"Yes."

"No, not much pain. Groggy." That much was true; the anesthesia made him feel limp and sleepy. But he could force himself to mental alertness, and that was the important part. He would rather be in pain than be so doped up he didn't know what was going on around him. The barbiturate coma had been a nightmare of darkness, of *nothingness*, which he didn't want to experience again, even in a mild form. Even amnesia was better than that total lack of self.

"That's the last of it. No more surgery, no more tubes, no more needles. When the casts come off your legs, you can start getting back to your old shape." Frank had a quiet voice, and there was often a note of familiarity in it, as if they had known each other well.

His words touched a chord of recognition in Steve; his old shape hadn't been bulky muscles, but rather speed and stamina, a steely core of strength that kept him going when other men would have collapsed.

"Is Jay in any danger?" he asked, cutting through the cautious maneuvering to what was most important to him.

"Because of what you may have seen?"

"Yes."

"We don't anticipate any danger," Frank replied, his voice cautious. "You are important to us only because we need to know exactly what happened, and you might provide us with some answers."

Steve smiled wryly. "Yeah, I know. Important enough to cut through red tape and coordinate two, maybe three, separate agencies, as well as pulling in people from different branches of the service and from the private sector. I'm just an innocent bystander, aren't I? Jay may buy that, but I don't. So cut the crap and give me a yes or no answer. Is Jay in any danger?"

"No," Frank said firmly, and after a second Steve gave a fractional nod, all he could manage. Regardless of what Frank was hiding, he was still fond of Jay and protective of her. Jay was safe enough. Steve could deal with the rest later; Jay was what mattered now.

His legs were thin and weak after having been en-cased in plaster for six weeks; he ran his hands down them, getting himself accustomed to their peculiar lightness. He could move them, but his movements were jerky and uncontrolled. For the past couple of days he had been sitting in a wheelchair or in the bedside chair, letting his body adjust to movement and different pos-tures. His hands had healed enough that he had been able to stand, using a walker for support, for a few minutes each day. His store of knowledge was increas-ing all the time. He now knew that even when he was bent forward to hold the walker, he was several inches taller than Jay. He wanted to take her in his arms and hold her against him, to feel her soft body adjust to his size as he bent his head to kiss her. He'd been holding off, taking it slow, but now that was at an end.

Jay watched him massage his thighs and calves, his long fingers kneading the muscles with sure strokes. He was scheduled for a session in physical therapy that afternoon, but he wasn't waiting for someone else to do the work for him. He had been like a coiled spring since the surgery on his eyes: tense, waiting, but under iron control. It had been a month and a half since the explosion, and perhaps lesser people would still have been lying in bed and taking pills for the pain, but Steve had been pushing himself from the moment he'd regained consciousness. His hands had to be tender, but he used them and never winced. His ribs and legs had to hurt, but he didn't let that stop him. He never complained of a headache, though Major Lunning had told Jay he would probably have headaches for several months.

She glanced at her watch. He'd been massaging his legs for half an hour. "I think that's enough," she said firmly. "Don't you want to go back to bed?"

He straightened up in the wheelchair and his teeth flashed in a grin. "Baby, I'm so tired of that bed, the only way you could get me back in it would be if you crawled in there with me."

He looked so wickedly masculine that she felt herself weakening even as she tried to warn herself against his charm. He wasn't above using his appeal as a wounded warrior to get to her, blast his hide. She couldn't even look at him without getting wobbly kneed, and sometimes the way she felt about him welled up in her like a flood tide, pleasure and pain so sharply mingled that she would almost moan aloud. Every day he was stronger; every day he conquered new territory, exerted his will over another aspect of his life. It was both amazing and frightening to watch him and to realize the extent of his willpower as he dealt with his situation. He was so fiercely controlled and determined that it was almost inhuman, but at the same time he let her see how very human he was; he depended on her now more than she had ever imagined possible, and the vulnerability he revealed to her was all the more shattering because she knew how rare it was.

"Get the walker for me," he ordered now, turning his bandaged eyes toward her expectantly, as if waiting for her to protest.

Jay pursed her lips, looking at him, then shrugged and placed the walker in front of him. If he suffered a setback, it would be his own fault for refusing to accept his limitations. "All right," she said calmly. "Go ahead and fall. Break your legs again, crack your head open again and spend a few more months in here. I'm sure that will thrill the nurses."

He chuckled at her acerbity, a reaction that was becoming more frequent as he healed. He regarded it as a measure of his recovery; while he had been ill and helpless, she hadn't refused him anything. He liked finding this bite to her personality. A passive woman wouldn't suit him at all, but Jay suited him in every way, at all times.

"I won't fall," he assured her, levering himself into an upright position. He had to support most of his weight on his arms, but his feet moved when he told them to. Jerkily, true, but on command.

"And heee's offf aaand *stumbling*!" Jay cried in dry imitation of a racetrack announcer, her irritation plain.

He gave a shout of laughter and did stumble, but caught himself with the walker. "You're supposed to guide me, not make fun of me."

"I refuse to help you push yourself too hard. If you fall, it will be your own fault."

A crooked smile twisted his lips and her heart speeded up at the roguish charm it gave his face. "Ah, baby," he cajoled. "I'm not pushing too hard, I promise. I know how much I can do. Come on, guide me down the hall."

"No," she said firmly.

Two minutes later she was walking slowly by his side as he maneuvered the walker, and his reluctant legs, down the hall. At the end of the corridor, the Navy guard watched alertly, examining everyone and everything. It was like that every time Steve left his room, though he didn't realize he was guarded so closely. Jay felt a chill as her eyes met those of the guard and he nodded politely; no matter how calm everything seemed, the guards' presence reminded her that Steve had been involved in something highly dangerous. Wouldn't his amnesia put him in even more danger? He didn't even know he was being threatened or by whom. No wonder those guards were necessary! But realizing just how necessary they were terrified her. This was all part of the large gray area Frank hadn't explained, but she knew it was there.

"This is far enough," Steve said, and cautiously turned around. He turned exactly 180 degrees and took two steps before stopping, his head turning back to her. "Jay?"

"Sorry." Hastily she moved to his side. How had he known how far to turn? Why wasn't he more uncertain of his movements? He walked slowly, still supporting most of his weight on his arms and hands, but he seemed deliberate and sure. He was slowed by his injuries but not thwarted. He wouldn't let himself give in; he didn't look on his injuries as something to be recovered from, but rather as something to be conquered. He would handle this on his own terms, and win, because he wouldn't accept anything less.

She saw even more of his determination in the following days as he sweated through physical therapy. The therapist tried to restrain him but Steve insisted on setting his own pace. He swam laps, guiding himself by Jay's voice, and walked endlessly on a treadmill. By the third day of therapy he had discarded the walker permanently and replaced it with Jay. Grinning as he put his arm around her shoulder, he explained that at least she'd cushion him if he fell.

He had gained weight rapidly since the tube had been taken out of his throat, and now he regained his strength just as rapidly. Jay felt as if she could see a difference in him from one day to the next. Except for the bandages over his eyes, he seemed almost normal, but she knew every scar hidden by the comfortable sweats Frank had brought him to wear. His hands were still pink from the burns, and his ruined voice would never be much better. Nor was his memory showing any sign of returning. There were no flashes of memory or glimmers of recognition. It was as if he had been born when he had fought his way out of unconsciousness to respond to her voice, and nothing existed before that.

Sometimes, watching him as he exercised with that frightening relentlessness of his, she caught herself hoping that his memory *wouldn't* return, and then guilt would eat at her. But he depended on her so much now, and if he began to remember, the closeness between them would fade. Even as she tried to protect herself from that closeness, she treasured every moment and wanted more. She was caught on the horns of her own dilemma and couldn't decide how to get free. She could protect herself and walk away, or she could grab for whatever she could get, but she couldn't decide to do either. All she could do was wait, and watch over him with increasing fierceness.

The day the bandages were supposed to come off his eyes, he got up at dawn and prowled restlessly around the hospital room. Jay had gotten there early, feeling as anxious as he did, but she forced herself to sit still. Finally he turned on the television and listened intently to the morning news, a frown knitting his brow.

"Why the hell doesn't that damn doctor hurry up?" he muttered.

Jay looked at her watch. "It's still early. You haven't even had breakfast yet."

He swore under his breath and raked his fingers through his hair. It was still shorter than was fashionable, but long enough to cover the scar that bisected his skull, and it was dark and shiny, undulled by sunlight, and beginning to show a hint of waviness. He prowled some more, then stopped by the window and drummed his fingers on the sill. "It's a sunny day, isn't it?"

Jay looked out the window at the blue sky. "Yes, and not too cold, but the weather forecast says we could have some snow by the weekend."

"What's the date?"

"January 29."

His fingers continued to tap against the sill. "Where are we going?"

Jay felt blank. "Going?"

"When they release me. Where are we going?"

She felt a shock like a slap in the face as she realized he would be released from the hospital within a few hours if everything was all right with his eyes. The apartment Frank had rented for her was tiny, only one bedroom, but that wasn't what alarmed her. What if Frank intended to whisk Steve away from her? Granted, he had once said something about her staying with Steve until his memory returned, but it hadn't been mentioned since. Was that still his plan? If so, where did he intend for Steve to live?

"I don't know where we'll go," she replied faintly. "They may want to send you somewhere...." Her voice trailed off into miserable silence.

"Too damn bad if they do." He turned from the window, and there was something lethal in his movement, a predator's grace and power. She stared at him, silhouetted against the bright window, and her throat contracted. He was so much harder than he had been that it almost frightened her, but at the same time, everything about him excited her. She loved him so much that it hurt, deep inside her chest, and it was getting worse.

A nurse brought in his breakfast tray, then winked at Jay. "I noticed you were here early, so I had an extra tray sent up. I won't tell if you won't." She brought in another breakfast tray, smiling as Jay thanked her. "This is the big day," the nurse said cheerfully. "Call this a sort of precelebration meal."

Steve grinned. "Are you that anxious to get rid of me?"

"You've been an absolute angel. We're going to miss those buns of yours, but hey, easy come, easy go."

A slow flush reddened Steve's cheeks, and the nurse laughed heartily as she left the room. Jay snickered as she unwrapped his silverware and arranged everything on the tray as he was accustomed to finding it.

"Bring your gorgeous buns over here and eat your breakfast," she ordered, still snickering.

"If you like them, get a good view," he invited, turning around and lifting his arms so she did indeed have an excellent view of his tight, muscular buttocks. "I'll even let you touch."

"Thank you, but food wins out over your backside. Aren't you hungry?"

"Starved."

They made short work of the meal, and soon he was again prowling about the small room, his restlessness making it seem even smaller. His impatience was a palpable force, bristling around him. He had spent too many weeks flat on his back, totally helpless and blind, unable even to feed himself. Now he had his mobility back, and in an unknown number of minutes he'd know if his sight had been restored. The doctor was certain of the surgery's success, but until the bandages were off and he could actually *see*, Steve wouldn't let himself believe it. It was the waiting and the lack of certainty that ate at him. He wanted to see. He wanted to know what Jay looked like; he wanted to be able to put a face to the voice. If he never saw anything else, he needed to see her face, if only for a moment. Every cell in his body knew her, could sense her presence; but even though she had described herself to him, he needed to have her face in his mind. The rest of his vanished memory didn't haunt him nearly as much as the knowledge of Jay that he'd lost, and the most piercing of all was that he couldn't remember her face. It was as if he'd lost a part of himself.

His head came up like a wary animal's as he heard the door open, and the eye surgeon laughed. "I half expected you to have taken the bandages off yourself."

"I didn't want to steal your thunder," Steve said. He was standing very still.

Jay was just as still, tension coiling in her as she watched the surgeon, a nurse, Major Lunning and

Frank all enter the room. Frank was carrying a bag with the name of a local department store on it, and he placed it on the bed. Without asking, Jay knew it contained street clothes for Steve, and she was vaguely grateful to Frank for thinking of it, because she hadn't.

"Sit down here, with your back to the window," the surgeon said, directing Steve to a chair. When Steve was seated, the doctor took a pair of scissors, cut through the gauze and tape at Steve's temple and carefully removed the outer bandage in order not to disturb the pads over his eyes or let the tape pull at his skin. "Tilt your head back a little," he instructed.

Jay's nails were digging into her palms and her chest hurt. For the first time she was seeing his face without bandages; even the relatively small swathe of gauze that had anchored the pads to his eyes had covered his temples and eyebrows, as well as his cheekbones and the bridge of his nose. He had been a handsome man, but he wasn't handsome any longer. His nose wasn't quite straight, and they had made the bridge a little higher than it had been before the explosion. His cheekbones looked more prominent. All in all, his face had more angles than it had before; the battering he'd taken was evident.

Slowly the doctor removed the gauze pads, then wiped Steve's eyes with some sort of solution. Steve's lids looked a little bruised and his eyes were deeper set than before.

"Pull the curtains," the doctor said quietly, and the nurse pulled them across the window, darkening the room. Then he turned on the dim light over the bed.

"All right, now you can open your eyes. Slowly. Let them get accustomed to the light. Then blink until they focus."

Steve opened his eyes to mere slits and blinked. He tried it again.

"Damn, that light's bright," he said. Then he opened his eyes completely, blinked until they were focused and turned his head toward Jay.

She sat frozen in place and her breath stopped. It was like looking into an eagle's eyes, meeting the fierce gaze of a raptor, a high-soaring predator. They were the eyes of the man she loved so much she ached with it, and terror chilled her blood. She remembered velvety, chocolate-brown eyes, but these eyes were a dark yellowish brown, glittering like amber crystal. An eagle's eyes.

He was the man she loved, but she didn't know who he was, only who he wasn't.

He wasn't Steve Crossfield.

Chapter Seven

His heart almost stopped in his chest. Jay. The face to go with the name and the voice, the gentle touch, the sweet and elusive scent. Her description of herself had been accurate, yet it was far from reality. The reality of Jay was a heavy mane of honey-brown hair, eyes of deep-ocean blue and a wide, soft, vulnerable mouth. God, her mouth. It was red and full, as luscious as a ripe plum. It was the most passionate mouth he'd ever seen, and thinking of kissing it, of having those lips touch his body, made a hard ache settle in his loins. She was immobile, her face colorless except for the deep pools of her eyes and that wonderful, exotic mouth. She stared at him as if mesmerized, unable to look away.

"How does everything look?" the surgeon asked. "Do you see halos of light, or are the edges fuzzy?"

He ignored the doctor and stood, his gaze never wavering from Jay. He would never get enough of looking at her. Four steps took him to her, and her eyes widened even more in her utterly white face as she stared up at him. He tried to make his hands gentle as he caught her arms and pulled her to her feet, but anticipation and arousal were riding him hard, and he knew his fingers bit into her soft flesh. She made an incoherent sound; then his mouth covered hers and the erotic feel of her full lips made him want to groan. He wanted to be alone with her. She was shaking in his arms, her hands clutching the front of his shirt as she leaned against him as if afraid she might fall.

"Well, your sense of direction is good," Frank said wryly, and Steve lifted his head from Jay's, though he kept her tight against him, her head pressed into his shoulder. She was still trembling violently.

"I'd say his priorities are in order, too," Major Lunning put in, grinning as he looked at his patient with a deep sense of satisfaction. It hadn't been too many weeks since he'd had serious doubts that Steve would live. To see him now, like this, was almost miraculous. Not that he was fully recovered. He still hadn't regained his full strength, nor had his memory shown any signs of returning. But he was alive, and well on the road to good health.

"I can see everything just fine," Steve said, his voice raspier than usual as he looked around the hospital room that had been home to him for more days than he cared to remember. Even it looked good. He'd disciplined himself to picture everything in his mind, to form a sense of spatial relations so that he always knew where he was in the room, and his mental picture had been remarkably correct. The colors were oddly shocking, though; he hadn't pictured colors, only physical presences.

The surgeon cleared his throat. "Ah . . . if you could sit down for a moment, Mr. Crossfield?"

Steve released Jay, and she shakily sat down, gripping the arms of the chair so tightly that her knuckles were white. They were wrong! He wasn't Steve Crossfield! Shock had kept her mute, but as she watched the surgeon examine Steve—no, *not* Steve!—control returned and she opened her mouth to tell him what a horrible mistake had been made.

Then Frank moved, tilting his head to watch the surgeon, and the movement caught her attention. Ice spread in her veins, freezing her brain again, but one thought still formed: if she told them that she'd made a mistake, that this man wasn't her ex-husband, they would have no use for her. He would be whisked away, and she would never see him again.

She began to shiver convulsively. She loved him. She didn't know who he was but she loved him, and she couldn't give him up. She needed to think this through, but she couldn't right now. She needed to be alone, away from watching eyes, so she could deal with the shock of realizing that Steve . . . dear God, Steve was dead! And this man in his place was a stranger.

She stood so abruptly that her chair tilted back on two legs before clattering forward again. Five startled faces turned to her as she edged toward the door like a prisoner trying to escape. "I . . . I just need some coffee," she gasped in a strained voice. She darted out the door, ignoring Steve's hoarse call.

He wasn't Steve. He wasn't Steve. The simple fact was devastating, rocking her to the core.

She ran down the hall to the visitors' lounge and huddled on one of the uncomfortable seats. She felt both cold and numb, and faintly sick, as if she were on the verge of throwing up.

Who was he? Taking deep breaths, she tried to think coherently. He wasn't Steve, so he had to be the American agent Frank had been so concerned about. That meant he had been deeply embroiled in the situation, the one man in the world who knew what had happened, if only he regained his memory. Could he be in danger if anyone—perhaps the person or persons who had set off the explosion that had already almost killed him—knew he was still alive? Until he recovered his memory, he couldn't recognize his enemies; his best protection now was the false identity he wore. She couldn't put him in more danger, nor could she give him up.

It was wrong to pretend he was someone he wasn't. By keeping this secret she was betraying Frank, whom she liked, but most of all she was betraying Steve...*damn*, she hated calling him that, but what else could she call him? She had to continue thinking of him as Steve. She was betraying him by putting him in a life that wasn't his, perhaps even hindering his complete recovery. He would never forgive her when he knew, if he ever regained his memory. He would know she had lied to him, that she had forced him to live a lie by putting him in her ex-husband's place. But she couldn't put him at risk. She just couldn't. She loved him too much. No matter what it cost her, she had to lie to protect him.

"Jay."

It was *his* voice, the raw, gravelly voice that haunted her at night in the sweetest of dreams. Numbly she turned her head and looked at him, still so shocked that she couldn't guard her expression. She loved him. Loving Steve, with his need for excitement that she couldn't

She panicked all over again. Home? Were they expecting her to take him to the small one-bedroom apartment she'd been using for the past two months? Or would they take him away from her after all, to finish recuperating in some unknown place?

They left the lounge to find Frank leaning patiently against the wall, waiting for them. He straightened and smiled, but his eyes were sympathetic as he looked at Jay. "Feeling better now?"

She took a deep breath. "I don't know. Tell me what's going to happen, then I'll tell you how I feel."

Steve put his arm around her waist. "Don't worry, sweetheart. They're not sending me anywhere without you. Are you, Frank?" He asked the question mildly, but there was steel underlying his tone, and his yellow-brown eyes narrowed.

Frank looked back at him with wry humor. "It never even crossed my mind. Let's step back into your room and we'll talk."

When they were once again behind a closed door, Frank walked over to the window, opened the curtains and looked out, blinking a little at the brightness of the winter sun. "First, you have to let the surgeon finish his examination of your eyes," he said, and glanced back at Steve. "And you'll need a follow-up exam next week, but I'll arrange that."

Steve made an impatient gesture, one that Frank read perfectly. He held up both hands, palms out in a delaying motion. "I'm getting to that. We'd like to keep you safe, but accessible to us. If you agree, we plan to move you to a safe house in Colorado."

Jay's head spun, and she sat down abruptly. Colorado? Her life had been turned upside down in the past two months, so the thought of such a drastic change shouldn't have stunned her, but it did. How could she go off to Colorado? Then she looked at Steve and knew she would go anywhere if it meant she could be with him. It was ironic. When she had been married, the most important thing in her life had been to establish some sort of stability on which to build her relationship with Steve, and the marriage hadn't survived. Now she had to pretend this man was Steve, but she was willing to walk away from everything and everyone she knew just to be with him. Painful sadness filled her, because this pointed out so clearly that she hadn't truly loved the real Steve Crossfield, though she had wanted to. He had held her away, walked his path alone and died alone without anyone ever really being close to him.

"Denver?" Steve guessed.

"No. The closest town is forty miles from the cabin by road, about fifteen air miles. It's a quiet, peaceful place, with no one to put any pressure on you."

"It's really nice of you folks to do all of this, just for the chance to talk to me when I get my memory back," he drawled, watching Frank with a hard gleam in his eyes.

Frank laughed, thinking that some things never changed. Even without his memory, he was so sharp he'd already put part of the puzzle together. "Why don't you go to the apartment and start packing?" Frank suggested to Jay, then lifted his brows in question. "If you want to go, that is."

"She's going," Steve said flatly, crossing his arms as he leaned against the bed. "Or I don't go."

Because she desperately needed the chance to be alone and think, Jay said yes. She slipped from the room without looking at either man, afraid they would see the terror in her eyes.

Steve regarded Frank in silence for a moment before growling, "You told me there wasn't any danger. Why the safe house?"

"So far as we know, you aren't in any danger—"

"Look, you can cut the crap," he interrupted. "I was an agent. I know all of this—" he gestured at the hospital surrounding him "—wasn't done out of the goodness of the government's heart. I know those guards aren't out there for decoration. I also know you wouldn't go to the expense of hiding me away in a safe house unless there was some threat to me, and unless you very badly need some information I may have."

Frank looked interested. "How did you know the guards were there?"

"I heard them," Steve replied shortly.

Now what? Frank looked at the man who had been his friend for over a decade and wondered how much to tell him. Not all of it, for damned certain. Until the Man nailed Piggot, the masquerade had to continue because it was Steve's best protection against any more attacks on his life. He knew too much for them to leave anything about his security to chance, and for the masquerade to be complete, it had to include Jay. The Man didn't take chances with his agents, or his friends, and Steve was both.

"You're right," Frank said. "You're an agent. A very highly trained agent, and we think the information you got on your last assignment is critical."

"Why the safe house?" Steve asked again, not letting up.

"Because the guy who tried to blow you to kingdom come went underground and hasn't surfaced yet. Until we get him, we want to make certain you're safe."

Like a burst of lightning, fury turned his eyes to yellow. "And you dragged Jay into this?"

Frank watched him warily, knowing how fast he could move. "Piggot doesn't know anyone survived the explosion. We just don't want to take any chances with you."

The yellow eyes flickered at the mention of Piggot's name. "Piggot. What's his first name?"

"Geoffrey."

Again there was that flicker in Steve's eyes and Frank watched closely, wondering if the mention of Piggot's name would trigger any real memory. But if it did, Steve kept it to himself. "I want to see the file you have on him," he said.

"I'll see if I can get clearance."

"But don't expect it, right? I'm a security risk now."

"That's the way it's played."

"Yeah. Now tell me why you had to bring Jay into the game. She doesn't know I'm an agent, does she?"

"No. We brought her in to identify you. It's as simple as that. And once she was here . . . you responded to her voice so strongly that the doctors decided it would help you to have her around. So she stayed." That was the truth, as far as it went. Frank just hoped Steve wouldn't ask too many more questions. He'd told him about all he could without clearance from the Man.

Steve rubbed his jaw as he mentally cataloged what Frank had told him. If he'd felt his presence was endangering Jay, he would have walked away from her that minute, but he felt Frank's sincerity. The other man thought they were safe enough. The deciding factor was the thought of living in an isolated house with Jay, just the two of them. He would have another chance. He would learn again what pleased her, and what made her angry. They would have another first time together. After he got all his strength and stamina back, they would lie in bed on cold, snowy mornings and make love until their bodies were damp with sweat even in the chilled air, and she would give him all the fiercely passionate love he could sense inside her. She presented a calm, controlled facade to the world, but perhaps because he hadn't been able to see her and had been forced to rely on his other faculties, he'd sensed the depth of her emotions behind that cool control. Maybe he'd been fool enough to let her slip away from him before, but not again.

"Okay," he said, exhaling slowly. "So we go to this safe house. What kind of security and communications does it have?"

"Bulletproof windows, reinforced steel doors. The cabin is isolated, built on a high meadow. There aren't any roads going up there, so a four-wheel-drive vehicle will be made available to you. The cabin has its own generator, so there aren't any public utility records. You're connected to a satellite-dish antenna for communication and entertainment, with both computer and radio-sending capabilities."

Steve's expression was remote as he concentrated, considering the angles. "Are there any active security systems, or just the passive precautions?"

"Just the passive."

"Why not thermal or motion sensors?"

"To begin with, this cabin is so safe it isn't even on file. And there's a lot of wildlife in the area, which would constantly trigger the alarms. We could set up a perimeter of thermal sensors and program the system to sound the alarm only at a large heat source, but a deer would still set it off."

"How inaccessible is this place?"

"There's just one track leading to it, and I'm being kind by calling it a track. It winds from the cabin across the meadow and down a mountain before it hits a dirt road, then it's twenty more miles before the dirt road runs into a paved secondary road."

"Then a laser across the track would alert us to most visitors, while almost eliminating alarms triggered by wildlife, by covering only a thin strip of the track."

Frank grinned. "You know, don't you, that a bunny is going to hop through that light beam and set off the alarm? All right, I'll have a laser alarm system set up. Do you want an audible or visual alarm?"

"Audible, but a quiet one. And I want a portable beeper to carry with me when we have to leave the house."

"For someone with amnesia, you sure remember a lot," Frank murmured as he took a small pad from his inside coat pocket and began making notes.

"I remember the names of the heads of state of just about every country in the world, too," Steve replied. "I've had a lot of time to play mind games with myself, putting together pieces of the puzzle by cataloging the things I know. I lost everything personal, but I kept a lot of the things related to my job."

"Your job meant a lot to you. It does that, sometimes, takes over so much that the personal side of life kind of fades away."

"Has it done that for you?"

"It did once, a long time ago. Not now."

"How did you get involved in this? You're FBI, and this sure as hell isn't a Bureau operation."

"You're right about that. A lot of strings were pulled, but there are a few people with the power to manage it."

"Very few. So I'm CIA?"

Frank smiled. "No," he said calmly. "Not exactly."

"What the hell does that mean, 'not exactly'? I'm either CIA or I'm not. There's a shortage of alternatives."

"You're affiliated. That's all I can say, other than to assure you that you're perfectly legal. When you recover your memory you'll know why I can't say more."

"All right." Steve shrugged his acceptance. It didn't really matter. Until he regained his memory, the knowledge wouldn't do him any good.

Frank indicated the bag he had brought in with him. "I brought street clothes for you to change into, but first let me get the surgeon in here to finish your exam. After that, I guess you'll be released."

"I'll need more clothes before we go to Colorado. By the way, where did I live?"

"You have an apartment in Maryland. I've arranged for your clothes to be packed and carried to the plane, but they won't fit until you've gained back the weight you've lost. You'll need new clothes until then."

Steve grinned, feeling suddenly light-spirited. "Jay and I will both need new clothes. The snow in Colorado is probably ass-deep to a giraffe."

Frank threw back his head and laughed.

Jay sat on the bed in the cramped apartment she'd been using for the past two months. Her heart was pounding and chills kept racing up and down her spine.

The implications, and complications, of the situation terrified her.

Now she knew what it was that had been bothering her off and on for two months; what she had never been able to put her finger on before. When she had been brought here and asked to identify the man in the bed, she hadn't been able to positively say he was Steve Crossfield. Then Frank had said that the man had brown eyes, and she had based her identification on that, because Steve had had dark, velvety eyes, "Chrissy eyes." Probably to a man, or on a vital statistics sheet, brown eyes were simply brown eyes. They didn't allow for chocolate brown, hazel brown or fierce yellow-brown. *But Frank had known that the man had brown eyes!*

She pressed her hands to her temples and closed her eyes. Frank must have known the color of his own agent's eyes, and he had known that Steve's eyes were brown, so it followed that Frank had also realized she couldn't base her identification simply on eye color, yet he had led her to do exactly that. She realized now that he had gently maneuvered her into declaring the man to be Steve Crossfield. He must have known there was at least a fifty-percent chance that the man wasn't Steve, so why had he done it?

The only answer she could come up with, and the one that terrified her, was that Frank had known all along that the man was the American agent and not Steve. He had taken Steve's identity and given it to the man, and given the tale substance by having Steve Crossfield's ex-wife confirm the identity, then maneuvered her into a bedside vigil that would have convinced anyone.

So Steve, the real Steve, was dead, and the agent had been given his identity for... protection?

It all fit. The plastic surgery on his face to alter his appearance; the bandaged hands to prevent fingerprints being taken. Had they done surgery to alter his fingerprints, too? Horrible thought: had they also deliberately damaged his larynx to change his voice? No, surely not. She couldn't believe that. All the doctors had fought so hard for his life, and Frank had been so anxious. No wonder. The man was probably Frank's friend!

But was the amnesia real? Or was the man faking it so he wouldn't have to "remember" any of the details of their supposed life together? Amnesia would be a convenient excuse.

She had to believe the amnesia was real, or she would go mad. She had to believe that "Steve" was as much in the dark as she was, maybe even more so. And Frank had been sincerely distressed when Major Lunning had told them about the amnesia.

So that left her back at the beginning. If she told Frank she knew Steve wasn't really Steve, the game would be up and they would have no more use for her. She was a screen, useful only to provide incontrovertible proof that the man who had survived the explosion was Steve Crossfield.

So she had to go along with the deception and continue pretending he was Steve, because she loved him. She had fallen in love with him before she even knew what he looked like; she had loved his relentless will, his refusal to give in to pain, to stop fighting. She loved the uncomplaining way he went about recovery and rehabilitation. Except for occasional frustration at his lack of memory, he hadn't let anything get him down. She had fallen in love with the man while he was stripped down to his basic character, without any of the camouflaging layers added by society.

She couldn't give him up now. Yet neither could she take him as hers; she was as caught in the web of circumstance as he was. He trusted her, but she was being forced to lie to him about something as basic as his identity. She knew the man, but she still knew nothing about his life. Dear God, what if he were married?

No, he couldn't be. Whatever game they were playing, they wouldn't tell a woman that she was now a widow, then give her husband another identity. Jay simply couldn't believe that of Frank. But there could still be a woman in Steve's life, someone he cared for, someone who cared for him, even though they weren't married. Was there such a woman waiting for him now, weeping because he'd been gone for so long, and she was terrified that he would never come back?

Jay felt sick; her only choices were twin prongs of the devil's pitchfork, and either would be pure torment. She could either tell him the truth and lose him, very possibly throwing him into danger, or she could lie to him and protect him. For the first time in her life she loved someone with the full force of her nature, with nothing held back, and her emotions propelled her toward the only choice she *could* make. Because she loved him, she could do nothing but protect him, no matter what the cost to herself.

Finally she got up and threw her clothing haphazardly into suitcases, not caring about wrinkles. Two months ago she had stepped into a hall of mirrors, and she had no way of knowing if the reflections she saw were accurate or a carefully constructed illusion. She thought of her chic apartment in New York and how much she had worried about losing it when she'd lost her job, but she couldn't think now why it had seemed so important to her. Her entire life had been thrown off kilter, and now it rotated on a different axis. Steve was the center of her life, not an apartment or a job, or the security she had fought so hard to win. After years of struggle she was throwing it all away just to be with him, and she had no regrets or moments of longing for that life. She loved him. Steve, yet not Steve. His name, but another man. Whoever he was, whatever he was, she loved him.

She found a box and dumped into it the few personal articles such as books and pictures that she'd brought to Washington. It had taken her less than an hour to get ready to leave forever.

As she went back and forth, loading things into the car, she looked around carefully, wondering if any of the people she could see supposedly going about their own business were in reality watching her. Maybe she was getting paranoid, but too much had happened for her to take anything for granted, even the appearance of normalcy. That very morning she had looked into fierce, golden eyes and realized that everything that had happened during the past two months had been a lie. The blinders of trust had been stripped from her eyes, making her wary.

Suddenly she felt a driving need to be with him again; uncertainty made her desperate for him. He was no longer a patient in need of her care and attention, but a man who, in spite of his memory loss, would be more surefooted than she was in this world of shifting reality. The instincts and reactions she had wondered about were now explained, as was the scope of his knowledge of world politics. He had lost his identity, but his training had remained with him.

He and Frank were lounging in the hospital room, patiently waiting for her. Jay barely managed a greeting for them; her eyes were on Steve. He had changed into khaki pants and a white shirt with the sleeves rolled back over his forearms. Even as lean as he was, he still gave the impression of power. His shoulders and chest strained at the cotton shirt. With the bandages gone from his eyes, he had shed the last semblance of being in need of care. He looked her over from head to foot and his eyes narrowed in a look of sexual intent as old as time. Jay felt it like a touch, stroking over her body, and she felt both warm and alarmed.

He got to his feet with lazy grace and came to her side, sliding his arm around her waist in a possessive gesture. "That was fast. You must not have packed much."

"It wasn't actually packing," she explained ruefully. "It was more like wadding and stuffing."

"You didn't have to be in such a hurry. I wasn't going anywhere without you," he drawled.

"Both of you have to go shopping, anyway," Frank added. "I didn't think of it, but Steve pointed out that neither of you has clothes suited to a Colorado winter."

Jay looked at Frank, at his clear, calm eyes and friendly face. He'd been a rock for her to lean on these past two months, smoothing the way for her, doing what he could to make her comfortable, and all the time he'd been lying to her. Even knowing that, she simply couldn't believe he'd done it for any reason other than to protect Steve, and because of that she forgave him completely. She was willing to do the same thing, so how could she hold it against him?

"There's no point in shopping here," Steve said. "Or even in Denver. If we go to a city, we'll have to get what some department-store buyer thinks is stylish for a winter vacation. We'll stop at some small-town general store and buy what the locals buy, but not at the town closest to the cabin. Maybe one about a hundred miles from it."

Frank nodded at that impeccable logic, as well as the ring of command in Steve's raspy voice. He was taking over the show, but then, they hadn't expected anything else; amnesia didn't change basic character traits, and Steve was an expert at logistics. He knew what to do and how to get it done.

Jay didn't exhibit any surprise at the precautions. Her deep blue eyes were calm. Having made her decision, she was ready for whatever happened. "Will we need any sort of weapon?" she asked. "After all, we'll be pretty isolated." She had the urbanite's distaste for guns and violence, but the thought of living on a remote mountain put things in a different light. There were times when guns were practical.

Steve looked down at her, and his arm tightened around her. He'd already discussed weapons with Frank. "A rifle wouldn't be a bad idea."

"You'll have to show me how to shoot. I've never handled a gun."

Frank checked the time. "I'll make a call and we'll get started. By the time we get to the airport, the plane will be ready."

"Which airport are we using?"

"National. We'll be flying in to Colorado Springs, then driving the rest of the way." Satisfied with the way things had turned out, Frank went to make his call. Actually he had to make two calls: one to the airport to have the plane readied, and another to the Man to bring him up-to-date.

Chapter Eight

After a series of small delays, it was midafternoon before the private jet actually took off from Washington National Airport, and the sun was already low in the pale winter sky. There was no way they could make it to the cabin that night, so Frank had already made arrangements for them to stay overnight in Colorado Springs. Jay sat by a window, her muscles tense as she looked down at the monochromatic scenery without really seeing it. She had the sensation of stepping out of one life and into another, with no bridge by which to return. She hadn't even told her family where she was going; though they weren't a close-knit group, they did usually know everyone's location. She hadn't seen any of them at Christmas because she had remained at the hospital with Steve, and now it was as if a tie had been severed.

Steve sat beside her, his long legs stretched out as he lounged in the comfortable seat and pored over several current news magazines. He was totally absorbed, as if he'd been starved for the written word. Abruptly he snorted and tossed his magazine aside. "I'd forgotten how slanted news coverage can be," he muttered, then gave a short laugh at his own phrasing. "Along with everything else."

His wry tone splintered her distracted mood and she chuckled. Smiling, he turned his head to watch her, rubbing his eyes to focus them. "Unless my vision settles down, I may need glasses to read."

"Are your eyes bothering you?" she asked, concerned. He'd worn sunglasses since leaving the hospital, but had taken them off when they had boarded the plane.

"They're tired, and the light is still too bright. It's a little hard to focus on close objects, but the surgeon told me that might clear up in a few days."

"Might?"

"There's a fifty-percent chance I'll need reading glasses." He reached over and took her hand, rubbing his thumb over her palm. "Will you still love me if I have to wear glasses?"

Her breath caught and she looked away. Silence thickened between them. Then he squeezed her hand and whispered roughly, "All right, I won't push. Not right now. We'll have time to get everything settled."

So he intended to push later, when they were alone in the cabin. She wondered exactly what he wanted from her: an emotional commitment, or just the physical enjoyment of her body? After all, it had been at least two months since he'd had sex. Then she wondered who had been the last woman to lie in bed with him, and jealousy seared her, mingled with pain. Did that woman mean anything to him? Was she waiting for him, crying herself to sleep at night because he didn't call?

They spent the night at a motel in Colorado Springs. Jay was surprised to find there was only a light dusting of snow on the ground, instead of the several feet she had expected, but random flakes were swirling softly out of the black sky with the promise of more snow by morning. The cold pierced her coat, and she shivered as she turned the collar up around her ears. She would be glad to get something more suitable to wear.

Steve was tired from his first day out of the hospital, and she was exhausted, too; it had been a hard day for both of them. She lay down across the bed in her room and dozed while Frank went to get hamburgers for dinner. They ate in Frank's room, and she excused herself immediately afterward. All she wanted was to relax and gather her thoughts. To that end she took a long, hot shower, letting the water beat the tension out of her muscles, but it was still hard to think coherently. The risk she was taking frightened her, yet she knew she couldn't go back. Couldn't—and wouldn't.

She tied the belt of her robe securely and opened the bathroom door, then froze. Steve was stretched out on her bed, his arms behind his head as he stared at the television. The picture was on, but the sound was off. She looked at him, then at the door to her room, her brows puckered in confusion. "I thought I locked the door."

"You did. I picked the lock."

She didn't move any closer. "A little something you remembered?"

He looked at her, then swung his legs off the bed and sat up. "No, I didn't remember it. I just knew how to do it."

Good Lord, what other suspicious talents did he have? He looked lean and dangerous, his battered face hard, his yellow eyes narrow and gleaming; he was probably capable of things that would give her nightmares, but she didn't fear him. She loved him too much; she had loved him from the moment she had first touched his arm and felt his will to live burning in him. But her nerves jangled as he stood and took the few steps he needed to reach her. He was so close now that she had to look up to see his face; she could feel the heat emanating from his body, smell the warm, musky male scent of his skin.

He cupped her cheek in his palm, his thumb rubbing lightly over the shadows fatigue had smudged under her eyes, making their blueness seem even deeper. She was pale and jittery, her body trembling. She had taken care of him for months, spending all day, every day, at his bedside, willing him to live and pulling him out of the darkness. She had filled his whole life to the point that even the shock of having amnesia paled in comparison. She had gotten him through hell. Now the strain was telling on her, and he was the stronger one. He could feel the tension in her, vibrating like a string at the point of breaking. He slid his arm around her waist and pulled her forward until her body rested against his. His other hand moved from her cheek into her heavy brown hair, exerting just enough pressure to bring her head against his shoulder.

"I don't think this is a good idea," she whispered, the sound muffled in his shirt.

"It *feels* like a damned good idea," he muttered. Every muscle in his body was tightening, his loins growing heavy with desire. God, he wanted her. His hands moved over her slender body. "Jay," he whispered roughly, and bent his head to hers.

The hot, needful pressure of his mouth made her dizzy. The stroking of his tongue against hers made her tighten inside with pleasure so piercing it was almost unbearable. Her hands lifted to the back of his neck, clinging as all strength washed out of her legs. She barely noticed as he turned with her still in his arms and forced her backward until the bed nudged against the backs of her knees. She lost her sense of balance, but his arms supported her as she fell back, and then his hard weight came down on top of her.

She had forgotten how the pressure of a man's body felt, and she inhaled sharply as quick response flooded her veins. The wide expanse of his chest flattened her breasts, and the swollen ridge of his manhood pushed against her feminine mound, his thighs controlling the restless movement of her legs. He kissed her again and again, barely letting her catch her breath before his mouth returned to take it away once more. Feverishly they strained together, wanting more. He pulled at the belt of her robe until the knot gave and the fabric parted, exposing the thinner fabric of her nightgown. He made a rough sound of frustration at this additional barrier, but for the moment he was too impatient to deal with it. His hand closed over her breast, kneading the soft flesh, his thumb making circles on her nipple until it tightened into a nub.

She whimpered softly into his mouth. "We can't," she cried, desperation and desire tearing her apart.

"The hell we can't," he rasped, taking her hand and moving it down his body to where his flesh strained at the fabric of his pants. Her fingers jerked at the contact; then a spasm of pain crossed her pale face, and her hand lingered involuntarily, exploring the dimensions of his arousal. He caught his breath. "Jay, baby, don't stop me now!"

She was stunned at how quickly passion had exploded between them; one kiss and they were falling on the bed. Her lips trembled as she stared up at him. She didn't even know his name! Tears burned her eyes and she blinked them away.

He groaned at the liquid sheen welling in her eyes and kissed her again with rough passion. "Don't cry. I know this is fast, but everything's going to be okay. We'll get married as soon as we can, and this time we'll make a go of it."

Shocked, she swallowed convulsively and barely managed to speak. "Married? Are you serious?"

"As serious as a heart attack, baby," he said, and grinned roguishly.

The tears burned again, and again she forced them back. Misery filled her. She wanted nothing more than to marry him, but she couldn't. She would be marrying him under false pretenses, pretending he was someone he wasn't. Such a marriage probably wouldn't even be legal. "We can't," she whispered, and a tear rolled out the corner of her eye before she could catch it.

He rubbed the wetness from her temple with his thumb. "Why can't we?" he asked with rough tenderness. "We did it before. We should be able to do better this time around, with our prior experience."

"What if you've remarried?" She gulped back a sob as she frantically thought up excuses. "Even if you haven't, what if there's someone else? Until you get your memory back, we won't *know!*"

He froze above her; then, with a sigh, he rolled off her to lie on his back, staring at the ceiling. He swore with a precise, Anglo-Saxon explicitness that was all the more jarring for the control in his voice. "All right," he finally said. "We'll get Frank to check it out. Hell, Jay, he's already checked it out! Isn't that why they had to get you to identify me?"

Too late she saw the trap, and saw also that he wasn't going to give up; with his usual steamroller determination, he was flattening the obstacles in his path. "You could still have some...someone who loves you, someone waiting for you."

"I can't promise you I don't," he said, turning his head to watch her with his predatory golden eyes. "But that's not a legal deterrent. I won't let you get away from me because some unknown woman somewhere may be in love with me."

"Until you get your memory back, you can't know that *you* aren't in love with someone else!"

"I *know*," he snapped, propping himself up on his elbow and leaning over her. "You keep coming up with excuses, but the real reason is that you're afraid of me, aren't you? Why? Damn it, I know you love me, so what's the problem?"

He was so arrogantly sure of her devotion that her own temper flared, but only for a moment. It was true. She had revealed it in a thousand different ways. She admitted shakily, "I do love you." There was nothing to be gained from denying it, and actually saying it aloud held its own painful sweetness.

His face softened and he put his free hand on her breasts, gently cupping them. "Then why shouldn't we get married?"

It was hard to concentrate with his palm burning her flesh through the thin cotton of her gown, and her body quickened again. She wanted him just as much as he wanted her, and denying him was the hardest thing she'd ever done, but she had no choice. Until his memory returned, she was in limbo. She couldn't take advantage of him now by marrying him under false pretenses.

"Well?" he demanded impatiently.

"I love you," she said again. Her lips trembled. "Ask me again when your memory has returned, and I'll say yes. Until then, until we're both certain it's what you want, I . . . I just can't."

His face hardened. "Damn it, Jay, I know what I want."

"We've been thrown together because of the circumstances! We don't know each other under normal conditions. You're not the same man I married—" how true that was! "—and I'm not the same woman. We need time! When your memory returns—"

"That's not guaranteed," he interrupted, his voice harsh with frustration. "What if my memory never returns? What if there's permanent brain damage? Then what? Are you still going to be saying no this time next year? Five years from now?"

"I don't think you have brain damage," she said shakily. "You recovered your speech and motor functions too easily."

"That's beside the damned point!" He was furious. Before she could move, he rolled onto her and pinned her hands to the bed. He was so close that she could see the yellow flecks in his irises, his curling black lashes, and a tiny scar in his left eyebrow she hadn't noticed before. He took a deep breath and slowly relaxed, the anger fading from him as he moved against the softness of her body, letting her feel his hardness. "I won't wait forever," he said in soft warning. "I'm going to have you. If not now, then later."

Then he rolled off her and was gone, moving with a peculiar silent grace that had become far more evident since the bandages had been removed from his eyes. There had been signs of it before, manifested in the superb control he had over his movements, but now it was striking. He didn't just move, he flowed, his muscles rippling with liquid power. Jay lay quietly on the bed, her body burning from frustration and the lingering sensation of contact with his, her eyes on the door he had closed behind him.

Who was he? Terror washed over her again, but it was terror for him. He was an agent, obviously, but not just any agent. He had clearly had extensive training; he was valuable enough that the government was willing to spend a fortune protecting him, as well as setting up this elaborate charade with her as an unsuspecting partner. If it hadn't been for his eyes, she might never have suspected a thing. But if he was that valuable to his own government, then logic told her he was of at least equal value to his enemies. All things were in proportion; whatever lengths had been taken to protect him, his enemies would be willing to go to equal lengths to find and destroy him.

As each new part of him was revealed, the stakes seemed to get higher. Now she knew that he was skilled at clandestine forced entry. She had picked up some of the lingo at Bethesda; what had she heard it called?

Light entry? No, soft entry. They called it a soft entry. Going in hard was an attack with weapons. Maybe the lock on the motel door wasn't the sturdiest model available, but she knew that picking it was beyond the average citizen. A good burglar wouldn't have any trouble with it, though . . . or a good agent.

And the way he moved. He was as controlled and graceful as a dancer, but a dancer's moves were poetic, while Steve's were evocative of silent danger.

His mind. No detail escaped him. He was trained to notice and use everything. Already Frank was deferring to him, another sign of his importance.

And he was in danger. Perhaps not immediate danger, but she knew it was there waiting for him.

The phone rang at two in the morning in Frank's room, and he muttered a sleepy curse as he fumbled for the receiver. It was second nature to him not to turn on a light, which could alert any outside observers that he was awake. Nor did he have to ask who it was, because only one man knew where they were.

"Yes," he said, and yawned.

"Piggot surfaced," the Man said. "East Berlin. We couldn't get to him in time, but we did find out that he's learned there was a survivor of the explosion and has made inquiries."

"Did the cover hold?"

"If Piggot asked at all, there has to be some doubt. Make certain your trail is covered. I don't want anyone other than the two of us to know where they are. How is he doing?"

"Better than I would have, if this had been my first day out of the hospital in two months. He's stronger than I expected. One other thing: I never would have believed it, but I think he's falling in love with her. It isn't just that he's been dependent on her, I think he's really serious."

"Good God," the Man said, startled. He laughed. "Well, it happens to the best of us. I have the final medical report on him here. His brain damage, if any, is minimal. He's a walking miracle, especially the speed of his recovery. He should regain his full memory but it may take a trigger of some sort to release it. We may have to bring his family in, or take him home, but not until we find Piggot. Until then, he stays hidden."

"The day we get Piggot, we tell him—and Jay—what's going on?"

The Man sighed. He sounded tired. "I hope he's recovered his memory by then. Damn it, we need to know what happened over there, and what he found out. But with his memory or without it, he has to stay there until we get Piggot. He has to be Steve Crossfield."

Steve woke early and lay in bed, feeling the fatigue that still weighted his body, as well as the sexual frustration that had been plaguing him for several weeks. He had tried, but even the rigorous exercise he'd been taking hadn't rebuilt his strength to the point he would have liked. Yesterday had exhausted him. He grinned sourly, thinking that it had probably been a good thing Jay had turned him down, because there was a good chance he would have collapsed on her in the middle of making love. Damn it.

He didn't intend to let her refusal stand in his way, but his lack of strength was something else. He had to get back in shape. It wasn't just that he was dissatisfied with his lack of strength and his physical limitations; he had a nagging feeling that he needed to be in top shape just in case . . . *what*? He didn't know what he expected to happen, but he had an uneasy feeling. If anything came up, he had to be in shape to protect Jay and handle the situation.

After getting out of bed, he first took the pistol that had been on the bedside table and placed it on the floor, within easy reach. Then he dropped down and began doing push-ups, counting silently. Thirty was his limit. Already panting, he rolled over and hooked his feet under the bed, his hands behind his head, and did sit-ups. The new scars on his abdomen throbbed at the strain he was putting on them, and sweat broke out on his brow. He had to stop at seventeen. Swearing in disgust, he looked down at his body. He was in pitiful shape. Before, he'd been able to do a hundred push-ups and sit-ups without even breathing hard— He went still, waiting for the half memory to become full-blown, waiting for the mental door to open, but nothing happened. Just for a second he'd had a glimpse of what his life had been before; then the door had closed again. The doctor had told him not to try to force it, but that blank door taunted him. There was something he needed to know, and rage built inside him because he couldn't force his way past the block.

Suddenly he heard footsteps outside the room, and he rolled, grabbing the pistol as he did so. Stretched out prone on the carpet, he aimed the pistol at the door and waited. The footsteps halted and a grumpy voice said, "June, come *on*. We need to get an early start and you've wasted enough time."

"Will the town be gone if we get there at four instead of three?" an equally grumpy female voice returned.

Steve let out his breath and climbed to his feet, staring at the pistol in his hand. It fit his palm as if he'd been born holding it. It was a Browning automatic, high caliber, and loaded with hollow-tip bullets that would make a hell of a hole going in and an even bigger one coming out. Frank had given it to him at the hospital while they were waiting for Jay to return and had told him to keep it on him, just as a precaution. When Steve had reached to take it, it was as if part of him had slipped back into focus. He hadn't realized how unusual it had been not to be armed, until the pistol was in his hand.

His reactions just now said a lot about the type of life he'd been living; it had been second nature for him to place the pistol within reach even while exercising, and second nature to regard those approaching footsteps as a possible danger. Maybe Jay had been smart to divorce him the first time. Maybe he wasn't doing her a favor by forcing his way back into her life, considering the dangers of *his*.

The pistol in his hand was a fine piece of hardware, but it couldn't compare to the feel of Jay's body. If he had to choose between Jay and his work, the job had just lost. He'd been a damned fool the first time, but he wasn't going to foul up this second chance. Whoever he worked for would just have to reassign him, bring him in, or he'd get out completely. No more clandestine meetings, no more assassins after him. Hell, it was time he settled down and let the Young Turks have their chance. He was thirty-seven, long past the age when most other men had wives and families.

But he wouldn't tell him until his memory returned, he thought cynically as he showered. Until then, he couldn't afford to totally trust anyone, except Jay.

* * *

They bought boots, socks and insulated underwear in Colorado Springs, jeans and flannel shirts in another town, hats and shearling coats in another. Jay also bought a thick down jacket with a hood, and a supply of long flannel gowns. The two vehicles Frank had obtained were four-wheel-drive Jeeps with snow tires, so they made good time, even though the snow became deeper the farther west they went.

Frank drove the lead Jeep, with Steve and Jay in the one behind. Jay had never driven a stick shift before, so the driving was left up to Steve. At first Jay worried about his legs, but he didn't seem to have any difficulty with the clutching and braking, so after a time she stopped worrying and began paying attention to the magnificent scenery as they drove west on U.S. 24. The sky, which had been clear, gradually became leaden with clouds, and occasional snowflakes began to drift down. The weather didn't worsen beyond that, and they continued to make good time even after they turned off onto a state highway. Then they left the state highway for a secondary road with much less traffic and a lot more snow, necessitating a slower speed. After that Frank took a dirt road that wound through the mountains for what seemed like hours, and finally he made another turnoff. Jay could see no discernible road or even a trail; they were simply driving up a mountain by the route of least resistance.

"I wonder if he knows where he's going," she muttered, clinging to the seat as the Jeep jolted to one side.

"He knows. Frank's a good agent," Steve returned absently, downshifting to climb a particularly steep rise. Once they reached the top, they seemed to be in a high, wide meadow that stretched and dipped for miles in front of them. They drove along the edge of the tree line until the meadow abruptly ended, and then they descended sharply down the side of the mountain. Next they climbed up another mountain, where there was a stretch of track barely wide enough to accommodate the Jeeps. On one side was the rock face, and on the other, nothing but an increasing distance to the bottom. Then they crested that mountain, too, and reached another rolling meadow. As the sun dipped behind the western peaks, Steve squinted his eyes at the tree line to their left. "That must be the cabin."

"Where?" Jay asked, sitting up eagerly. Just the thought of being able to get out of the Jeep and stretch her legs was pure heaven.

"In that stand of pines, just to the left."

Then she saw it and sighed in relief. It was just an ordinary cabin, but it was as welcome as a luxury hotel. It was tucked just under the trees, visible only from the front. Because it was built on a slope, the front was higher than the back; there were six wooden steps leading up to a porch that ran all the way across. Built onto the cabin at the back was a lean-to for the Jeeps, and thirty yards to the rear was a shed.

They parked under the lean-to and stiffly got out, arching their backs to stretch aching muscles. The air was so cold and crisp that it almost hurt to inhale, but the setting sun was painting the snowy peaks and ridges in shades of red, gold and purple, and Jay stood motionless, entranced, until Steve nudged her into motion.

It took several trips to carry everything in; then Frank took Steve to the shed to show him how the generator worked. Evidently someone had already been up to turn it on, because the electric lights worked and the refrigerator was humming. Jay checked the small pantry and refrigerator, and found them fully stocked with canned goods and frozen meats.

She gave herself a short tour of the cabin. Next to the kitchen was a small utility-mudroom with a modern washer and dryer. There was no dining room, only a round wooden table and four chairs in one corner of the kitchen. The living room was comfortably furnished in sturdy Early American, with brown corduroy upholstery. A brown-and-blue hooked rug covered the wooden floor, and one wall was almost entirely taken up by an enormous rock fireplace. There were two bedrooms of equal size, connected by the cabin's lone bathroom. Jay stared at the connecting door, her heart beating a little faster at the thought of sharing a bathroom with him. She knew the intimacy of damp towels hanging side by side, toiletries becoming jumbled together, a shared tube of toothpaste. His whiskers would be in the sink, his razor on the side. The small details of living together were at least as seductive as physical intimacies, meshing their lives at every moment of the day.

The back door slammed, and Steve called, "Where are you?" His rough voice was even raspier than usual from breathing the cold air.

"Exploring," she replied, leaving the bathroom and crossing to the bedroom door. "Any objections if I take the front bedroom? It has the best view."

A fire had already been laid in the fireplace. He bent down and struck a match on the hearth, then held it to the paper and kindling under the logs, not answering until he'd straightened. "Let me look at them."

Vaguely surprised, Jay stepped aside and let him enter. He examined the location of the windows and their locks, opened the closet and looked at it, then stepped into the adjoining bath.

"It's a connecting bath," she pointed out.

He grunted and opened the door into the second bedroom. The windows in both rooms were on the side walls, but because the rear of the cabin was closer to the ground than the front was, the windows in the second bedroom were more accessible from the outside. "All right," he said, checking the locks on his windows, too. "But I want it understood that if you hear anything at all during the night, you wake me. Okay?"

"Yes," she said, her throat constricting. All this was second nature to him. He must think there was some danger, too, despite all the precautions Frank had taken. She had wanted to think they were safe here, but perhaps they weren't. The best thing she could do was not argue with him.

He glanced at her, and his rough face softened a bit. "Sorry. I guess I'm overreacting to a strange situation. I didn't mean to scare you." Because the tension didn't fade from her eyes, he walked over to her, cupped her face in his hands, then kissed her. Her wonderfully full, lush, exotic mouth opened for him and his tongue teased at hers. Jay put her hands on his shoulders and luxuriated in the heat of his body against her. The cabin wasn't icy, but it was far from warm.

He held her against him for a moment, then reluctantly let her go. "Let's see what this place has in the way of grub. If I don't eat soon, I'm going to fall down." He wasn't exaggerating, she realized. She could feel a faint tremor in his muscles, a sign of the enormous strain he'd put on his body that day.

Casually she put her arm around his waist as they walked back to the living room. "I've already checked the food. We can have almost anything our hearts desire, as long as our hearts desire plain cuisine. If you want lobster or truffles, you're out of luck.''

''I'd settle for a can of soup,'' he said tiredly, and groaned as he sank down into one of the comfortable chairs. He stretched his legs out, absently rubbing his thighs.

''We can do better than that,'' Frank said as he brought in an armload of wood, having caught Steve's last comment. He stacked the wood on the hearth and dusted his hands. ''I think. I'm not much of a cook.'' He looked hopefully at Jay, and she laughed.

''I'll see what I can do. I'm a real whiz with microwave dinners, but I didn't see a microwave oven, so I'm a little lost.''

She was too tired to do much, but it didn't take a lot of effort to open two large cans of beef stew and heat them, or to brown buttered rolls in the gas oven. They were almost silent as they ate, and after Frank had helped her clean up the few dishes, they all took turns in the shower. By eight o'clock they were asleep, Jay and Steve in their respective bedrooms and Frank rolled in a blanket on the couch.

They rose early the next morning, and after a hearty breakfast Frank and Steve walked around in the snow. The gas stove and hot-water heater operated on butane gas, and the large tank had been filled; it shouldn't need refilling until spring. The fuel tank for the generator would need replenishing, but all Steve had to do was contact Frank by computer, and fuel would be brought in by helicopter. They didn't want a delivery to the cabin by any commercial business or utility, and, at any rate, the cabin was too difficult for an ordinary fuel truck to reach. It was a complicated setup, but it was meant to be an ultrasafe lodging, unlisted in any files. All in all, the place was stocked for a long-term stay, though Frank couldn't help wishing Steve would recover his memory soon and put an end to all this, or that Piggot would be caught.

"The nearest town is Black Bull, population one hundred thirty-three," Frank said. "Go down to the dirt road and turn right, and you'll eventually get there. It has a general store for basic food and supplies. If you want anything fancier, you'll have to find a larger town, but keep a low profile. You should have enough cash to last a couple of months, but let me know if you need more."

Steve looked out over the white meadow. The air was so clear, the early-morning sun so bright on the spotless snow, that it hurt his eyes. The cold burned his lungs. The land was so damned big and empty that it gave him an eerie feeling, but at the same time he was almost content. He was impatient for Frank to leave so he would finally be alone, completely alone, with Jay.

"You're safe here," Frank added. "The Man uses it sometimes." He glanced up at the cabin. "I wouldn't have brought Jay here if it wasn't safe. She's a civilian, so take good care of her, pal."

A tingle, a heightened awareness, had seized Steve when Frank mentioned the Man. It wasn't a sense of danger but a sort of excitement. The memory was there, but blocked from his consciousness by the lingering effects of the explosion. The Man was another piece of the puzzle.

He shook Frank's hand, and their eyes met in the comradeship of men who have been in danger together. "You probably won't see me again until this is over, but I'll be in touch," Frank said. "I'd better get moving. It's supposed to start snowing again this afternoon.''

They went inside and Frank got his gear, then told Jay goodbye. She hugged him, her eyes suspiciously bright. Frank had been her rock for two months, and she would miss him. He had also been a buffer between her and Steve; when he left, there would be only the two of them.

She glanced at Steve, to find him watching her intently. His pale brown eyes were glowing, yellower than they had moments before, like those of a raptor that had sighted its prey.

Chapter Nine

Jay had expected Steve to pounce on her, but to her relief he seemed to have other things on his mind. For the next week he spent the daylight hours prowling around the cabin and shed and exploring their high meadow, as tense and wary as a cat in unfamiliar surroundings. The hours passed tromping through the snow tired him, and as often as not he would go to sleep soon after eating dinner. Jay worried, until she realized that it was a natural part of his recovery. The rehabilitation he'd had in the hospital had given him a start, but he was still a long way from full strength, and the many hours of walking served two purposes: to acquaint him with his new territory, and to rebuild his stamina. It was the end of the week before he began to relax, but every day he still walked a perimeter around the cabin, watching, checking for any intrusion.

They seemed so isolated that she couldn't understand his caution, but she supposed it was ingrained in him. Watching him gave her an even greater insight into the man he was. He was so superbly suited to his occupation! He knew what to do by instinct, without needing to rely on memory.

When he was stronger, he began chopping wood to keep a good supply for the fireplace. They used the hearth for most of their heat, to conserve fuel. The cabin was so snugly built and insulated that it held heat well, and a good fire was sufficient to keep the entire place comfortable. At first his hands were sore and blistered, despite the gloves he wore, but gradually they toughened. After a while he added jogging to his activities, but he didn't jog in the meadow, where it was clear. He ran through the trees, up and down the hills, deliberately picking the roughest path, and every day his legs were a little stronger, his breathing a little easier, so he would push himself further.

Jay loved those first days in the cabin, high in the vast, silent meadow. Sometimes the only sound was that of the wind stirring the trees. Having been accustomed her entire life to the bustle of cities, the space and silence made her feel as if she'd been reborn in a new world. The last remnants of tension from her old life relaxed and faded away. She was alone in the mountains with the man she loved, and they were safe.

He began teaching her how to drive a stick shift. To Jay, it was fun, bouncing in the Jeep over the meadow. To Steve, it was a precaution, against the possibility that something could happen to him and Jay would have to do the driving. It might come down to a matter of saving her life.

There was a heavy snow the third week they were there. Jay woke early to a world where every sound had been muffled. She got up to peek out the window at the deep drifts of new snow, then tumbled back into her warm bed and fell instantly asleep again. When she woke the second time it was almost ten, and she felt wonderfully rested, as well as starving.

She dressed hurriedly and brushed her hair, wondering why the cabin was so silent. Where was Steve? She looked into his room, but it was empty. There was a pot of coffee in the kitchen, and she drank a cup while standing at the window, searching the tree line for some sign of him. Nothing.

Curious, she finished the coffee and returned to her room to stamp her feet into warm boots; then she put on her shearling coat and pulled a thick knit cap over her hair. It was unusual for Steve to go out without telling her where he would be and how long he'd be gone. She wondered what he was doing, and why he hadn't woken her. Could he have hurt himself?

Anxious now, she went down the back steps. "Steve?" she called softly, a little afraid to raise her voice. The meadow was so silent, and for the first time its isolation felt threatening, instead of safe. Was there someone else out there?

His footprints were plainly visible in the new snow. He'd evidently made several trips to the woodpile to replenish the supply in the house, because there was a worn trail between them; then he'd walked up the slope into the forest. Jay dug her gloves out of her coat pocket and put them on, and wished she'd wrapped a scarf around her nose and mouth. It was so cold that the air felt brittle. She turned the collar of the coat up around her neck and began following Steve's trail, carefully stepping in his tracks because that was easier than breaking through the snow herself.

The snow wasn't as deep under the trees, making the walking easier, but Jay kept to the prints Steve had made. The thickly-growing evergreens, their branches weighted down with snow, blanketed noise and muffled it out of existence. She could barely hear herself breathe or the snow crunching under her boots. She wanted to call Steve's name again but somehow didn't dare, as if it would be sacrilege in this silent white, black and green cathedral.

If anything, she tried to be even quieter, picking her way from tree to tree, trying to become part of the forest. Then, suddenly, she lost Steve's tracks. She stood under the drooping limbs of a spruce and looked around, but there were no more tracks to follow. It was as if he'd vanished. It was impossible to walk in the snow without leaving tracks! But there were no tracks under the trees. She looked up, wondering if he'd climbed a tree and was sitting there laughing at her. Nothing.

Common sense told her that he'd played some sort of trick, but his tracks would have to pick up somewhere. She thought a minute, then began walking in a slow, constantly enlarging circle. She would have to cross his path somewhere.

Fifteen minutes later, she was angry. Damn him! He was playing games with her, unfair games, considering his training. She was getting cold, and she was already starving. Let him play Daniel Boone; she was going back to the cabin to cook breakfast—for *one*!

Just to be perverse, she backtracked as cautiously as she'd come; maybe she could leave him in here, sneaking around and hiding from her while she was already back at the cabin, snug and warm and eating a hot breakfast. He'd show up after a while, all innocence, and he could damn well cook his own breakfast! Show-off!

She crept back toward the cabin, sidling as close to the tree trunks as she could, stopping often to listen for any betraying sound before moving to the next tree, and looking in all directions before moving again. Her indignation grew, and she began to think what she could do in the way of revenge, but most of her ideas seemed both petty and paltry. What she really wanted to do was hit him. Hard. Twice.

She had just begun to creep around a tree when the skin on the back of her neck prickled and she froze, her heart leaping in fear at the ancient warning of danger. She couldn't hear or see anything, but she could feel someone, or some*thing*, close by. Were there wolves in the mountains? Or bears? Motionless except for her eyes, she looked around for something to use as a weapon, and finally she saw the outline of a sturdy-looking stick, buried under the snow. A fraction of an inch at a time, she bent to reach for the stick, her senses raw and screaming.

Something hard and heavy hit her in the middle of the back, and another blow numbed her forearm. She was knocked facedown in the snow, her lungs straining for air, her arm useless. She couldn't even scream. She was jerked roughly onto her back, and there was a flash of shiny metal as a knife was laid against her throat.

Stunned, terrified, unable to breathe, she stared up into narrowed, deadly eyes as yellow as an eagle's.

His eyes widened as he recognized her, then narrowed again with rage. He jabbed the wicked-looking knife back into its scabbard and took his knee off her chest. "Damn it, woman, I could've killed you!" he roared, his voice like rusty metal. "What in hell are you doing?"

Jay could only gasp and writhe on the ground, wondering if she might die from lack of air. Her entire chest was burning and her vision was wavering.

Steve jerked her to a sitting position and whacked her on the back several times, hard enough to hurt, but at least the air rushed back into her body. She almost choked as her lungs expanded again, and tears sprang to her eyes. She gagged and coughed, and Steve patted her on the back but his tone was hard: "You'll be all right. It's less than you deserve, and a hell of a lot less than what could have happened."

She didn't plan it. She saw the stick out of the corner of her eye, the one she'd been reaching for when he'd hit her, and the next thing she knew it was in her hand. Red mist fogged her vision as she swung at him with all the strength her fury had given her. He dodged under the first blow, cursing, and leaped back to escape the second one. She moved to the left, trying to back him against a tree so he wouldn't be able to escape so easily, and swung again. He tried to grab the stick, and she caught him on the wrist with a solid *thunk*! then wound up for another blow. Cursing again, he bent low and rushed her. She hit him on the back with the stick just as his shoulder jammed into her stomach with enough force to knock her sprawling again.

"Damn it!" he yelled, kneeling astride her and pinning her wrists to the ground. "Settle down! Damn it, Jay! What in hell's wrong with you?"

She twisted and bucked beneath him, trying to throw him off. He tightened his knees on her sides, forestalling that effort, and his hands bit into her wrists so tightly there was no way she could free them. Finally she stopped struggling and glared impotently at him, her eyes like blue fire. "Get off me!"

"So you can brain me with that damn stick? Fat chance!"

She took a deep, shuddering breath and forced her voice to a relatively calm tone. "I won't hit you with the stick."

"Damn straight you won't," he grunted, releasing her hand to grab the stick and hurl it away from them. Jay used her free hand to wipe the snow out of her face, and slowly Steve eased his weight off her chest. She sat up and pulled the knit cap off her head to shake it free of snow.

Kneeling on one knee beside her, Steve brushed off her back. "Now suppose you explain just what you thought you were doing," he snapped.

Fury burst in her again and she swung at him. He jerked his head back in time to escape her fist, but the wet cap she held in her hand swiped his face with enough force to sting. Like a stroke of lightning she was flat on her back again. From between gritted teeth he said, "One more time and you'll eat standing up for a month!"

She blazed back at him: "You just try it! When I woke up and couldn't find you, I was worried you might be hurt, so I came looking for you. Then you started showing off with your Super Spy tricks, not letting me find you, until I got fed up and started back to the cabin. *Then* you knocked me down and pulled a knife on me, *and* yelled at me! You deserved to get hit with a stick!"

He glared down at her, taking in her tumbled hair and fierce blue eyes, and the stubborn set of those luscious

lips. He swore under his breath and thrust his fingers
into the honey-brown strands, holding her still while he
ground his mouth against hers. His kiss was half angry
and half starving. He was suddenly wild to feel her lips,
to put his tongue inside her mouth and taste her. She
kicked at him, and he moved swiftly, kneeing her legs
apart and settling himself between them, his weight
crushing her into the snow.

Jay groaned, and his tongue thrust into her mouth.
Suddenly she felt on fire, as her fury turned into a different, white-hot passion. Her hands were in his hair,
digging into his scalp as she returned his kiss as fiercely
as he gave it. His hips rubbed against her in primal
rhythm, thrusting as if to deny the sturdy denim between them, and her blood felt like lava.

Roughly he opened her thick coat and shoved the
edges aside, his hands covering her breasts, but still she
was protected from him by her shirt and bra, and the
contact wasn't enough. He jerked at her shirt, popping
three of the buttons off to be lost in the snow, and
opened it, too. The cold air rushed at her and she cried
out, but the sound was caught in his mouth. Her bra
had a front hook; he handled it easily and peeled the
thin cups away from her white, swollen breasts. Her
nipples were hard and tight from the cold, stabbing into
his palms when he put his hands over them.

He lifted his head. "Let me inside you," he rasped.
"Now." The need was riding him hard, just the way he
wanted to ride her. He put his hot mouth over a pout-
ing nipple and sucked strongly at it, rolling it around
with his tongue and listening to the incoherent sounds
of pleasure she made.

Jay thought she might die from wanting him, even
though he had scared her and hurt her; even though

he'd made her angrier than she could ever remember feeling at another human being. He'd loosed the passion that had always been in her nature, torn it out of her control. Her hands were shaking, her entire body was shaking, and she wanted more.

He lifted his mouth from her breast, and the shock of the cold air on her wet flesh was so painful she whimpered. Their eyes met, hers wide and dazed with the sudden passion, his narrow and burning, and she knew what he wanted, knew he was silently waiting for her permission. She knew that if she made the slightest sign of acquiescence he would take her there, in the cold and snow, and her entire body throbbed with the need to let him do just that. She started to whisper his name; then terror washed over her like freezing water and she stared up at his hard face as he waited for her answer. *She didn't know his name!* She could call him Steve, but he wasn't Steve. His face wasn't Steve's. She knew him and loved him, but he was a stranger.

He found his answer in the sudden rigidity of her body beneath him. He swore viciously as he got to his feet, one hand rubbing the back of his neck as if that could relieve his physical tension. Jay fumbled with her shirt, trying to draw the edges together, but the buttons were gone and her hands were shaking too badly, so finally she just fastened her coat and got to her feet. She had been burning up only moments before, but now she was freezing. She was covered with snow. She shook it out of her hair and dusted it off her jeans and coat as best she could, then retrieved her knit cap, but it had snow on it both inside and out, and would be worse than wearing nothing at all. Without a word, unable to look at him, she started toward the cabin.

He caught her roughly by the shoulder and swung her around. "Tell me why, damn it," he rasped.

Jay swallowed. She hadn't meant to stop him, and she couldn't explain the dreadful fear she lived with every moment, every day. "I've told you before," she finally managed. "They're good reasons." A single tear tracked down her cheek and formed frozen salt crystals before it reached her chin.

His face changed, some of the angry frustration leaving him, and he wiped at the tear with his gloved hand. "Are they? Your reasons don't make much sense to me. It's natural to want each other. How much longer do you think I can live like a monk? How much longer can you live like a nun? That's not my calling, baby, and damn it all to hell and back in a little red wagon, it's not as if it'll be the first time!"

She thought she would scream. She wanted to cry and she wanted to laugh, but neither would make sense. She wanted to tell him the truth, but the biggest fear she had was of losing him. So finally she did tell him the truth, or at least part of it. "It *will* be the first time," she croaked, strangling on the words. "This time. And it scares me."

She walked away again, and he let her go. She was shaking with cold by the time she got back to the cabin, and she took a long hot shower, then dressed in dry clothing. The smell of fresh coffee came from the kitchen, and she followed her nose to find him frying bacon and whipping eggs in a bowl. He had changed clothes, too, and she faltered under both his physical impact and a sudden realization. He was tall and muscular, as powerful as a puma, his shoulders and chest straining the seams of his shirt. In the weeks they had been there he'd gained weight and muscle, and his hair had grown enough that now it was a trifle long. He looked uncivilized and dangerous, and so utterly male that she quivered instinctively. He was no longer a patient. He had recovered both his health and his strength. She had followed him because she had been worried, but in her mind he had still been a wounded warrior. Now she knew that he wasn't. Her subconscious had recognized it earlier, when she had fought him. She never would have done that before.

He looked up at her, his gaze assessing. "I made fresh coffee. Drink a cup. You still look a little shaky. Does the thought of making it with me scare you that much?"

"*You* scare me." She couldn't stop the words. "Who you are. What you are."

An icy motionlessness seized him as he realized that she had guessed. "You said I was using Super Spy tricks."

"Yes," she whispered, and decided she did need that cup of coffee. She poured it and watched the steam rise for a moment before sipping. Why had she said that? She hadn't meant to. She was in agony, afraid that it would trigger his memory and he would leave, and equally afraid that he might never get his memory back. She was caught, trapped, because she couldn't call him hers until he regained his memory and *chose* her. If he would. He might just walk away, to his real life.

"I didn't think you knew," he said flatly.

Her head jerked up. "Do you mean you did?"

"There had to be more to it than the possibility that I had seen something before the explosion. The government doesn't work that way. I guessed, and Frank confirmed it."

"What did he say?" Her voice was thin.

His smile was equally thin, and a little savage. "That's about it. He can't tell me more because of the circumstances. I'm a security risk right now. How did you guess?"

"The same. There just had to be more to it."

"Is what I am the real reason you turned me down?"

"No," she whispered, an aching, needing expression in her eyes as she watched him. How could loving a man hurt so much? But it did, when the man was this one.

His entire body was taut, his mouth twisted. His voice was harsh. "Stop looking at me like that. It's all I can do to keep myself from pulling your pants off and laying you down on that table, and that isn't the way I want to take you. Not this time. So stop looking at me as if you'd melt if I touched you."

But I would, she thought, though she turned her eyes away. His words made her feel hot and shivery, thinking of the act he'd described, the scene forming in her mind. It would be raw and hot, and purely sexual. If he touched her, they would burn each other up.

He spent most of the day outside, but the tension between them didn't ease; it hung there, as thick and heavy as fog. When darkness finally drove him inside, his eyes burned her every time he looked at her. Instincts she hadn't known she possessed pulled her toward him, despite the reasons her mind presented for not letting their relationship progress. She lay alone in her bed that night, aching with the need to go to him and spend the long, dark hours in his arms. He was right; what did her reasons matter? It was already too late. She already loved him, for good or bad. That was the real danger, and it had been too late for a long time now. Keeping herself from him wouldn't lessen the pain if the worst happened and she lost him.

But she didn't go to him. Things often seemed different in daylight than when lying alone in the darkness, but caution wasn't what kept her in her own bed. Circumstances were hard enough; she had to call him by a name that wasn't his own, had to pretend he was someone else, but she wanted to be able to see his eyes when they made love. More than anything she wanted to know his real name, to be able to call him by it in her heart; failing that, she wanted to see his eyes, for they were his own.

A chinook blew in during the night, chasing away the weather system that had covered them with new snow. Mother Nature must have chuckled to herself as she promptly began melting the high white drifts with her hot winds, teasing them with a hint of a spring that was still over a month away. The melting snow dripped from the trees with a sound like rain, and there were crashes in the night as limbs dropped their white burdens.

The rise in temperature made Jay even more restless, and she was up at dawn. She could barely believe what she saw when she looked out. The hot wind had turned their winter wonderland into a wet, brown meadow dotted with shrinking patches of snow. The melting snow still dripped off the roof, and the heated air made her feel as if her skin would explode. How could it have happened so fast?

"A chinook," Steve said behind her, and she whirled, her heart jumping. She hadn't heard him approach, but he moved like a cat. He looked so ill-tempered that she almost stepped back. His eyes were hard and frosty, and a day's growth of beard darkened his jaw. He glanced from her to the window. "Enjoy it while you can. It'll feel like spring while we have it, and then it'll be gone, and the snow will come back."

They ate breakfast in silence, and he left the cabin immediately afterward. Later on in the morning, Jay heard the solid bite of the ax into wood, and she peeked out at him from the kitchen window. He had taken off his coat and was working in his shirt sleeves, which were rolled up over his forearms. Incredibly, sweat had left dark stains under his arms and down the center of his back. Was it that warm?

She walked out onto the front porch and lifted her face to the warm, sweet wind. It was incredible! Her skin tingled. The temperature was at least forty degrees higher than the day before, and the sun burned down from a cloudless blue sky. Suddenly her jeans and flannel shirt were much too heavy, and her skin began to glisten with moisture.

Like a child made giddy by spring, she hurried to her bedroom and stripped off her heavy, restricting clothes. She couldn't stand them another minute. She wanted to feel the air on her bare arms; she wanted to feel fresh and free, like the chinook. So what if winter could come back at any time? Right now, it was spring!

She pulled her favorite sundress from the closet and slipped it on over her head. It was white cotton, sleeveless, with a scoop neck, and far too flimsy for the temperature, which was probably only in the fifties, but it suited her mood perfectly. Some things were just meant for celebrating; this chinook was one of them.

She hummed as she began the preparations for lunch; it was a while before she noticed that Steve was no longer at the woodpile. If he'd gone off just at lunchtime, she would eat alone and he could do without! She still hadn't quite forgiven him for the day before.

Then she heard a slight noise from out front, and she removed the soup from the stove before walking to the front door. He'd pulled the Jeep around and was washing it. It was such a domestic scene that it lured her onto the porch, and she sat down on the top step to watch him.

He glanced up at her, and his eyes flickered over the dress. "Pushing it a little, aren't you?"

"I'm comfortable," she said, and she was. The crisp air was both chilly and warm, and the sun beating down on her was a delicious sensation. He'd given in to the rising temperature, too, by unbuttoning his shirt and pulling it out of his jeans.

She watched as he alternately scrubbed and rinsed, each time having to stop washing to take up the hose and spray the soap off the Jeep. Finally she went down to pick up the hose from where he'd dropped it. "You wash, I'll rinse."

He grunted. "Do you expect the same deal with the dishes?"

"Sounds fair to me. After all, I'm doing the cooking."

"Yeah, but I'm having to eat all that food so it won't go to waste."

She gave him an awful look. "Poor baby. I'll see what I can do to take that burden off you."

"Just like a woman. Tease her a little bit and she turns nasty. Some people just can't take a joke."

Jay turned the hose on the section of Jeep he'd just washed, but he didn't have time to step back, and the water hit the Jeep full blast, spraying back into his face and onto his clothes. He leaped back, swearing. "Damn it, watch what you're doing!"

"Some people just can't take a joke," Jay said sweetly, and turned the hose on him.

He yelled from the shock of the cold water hitting him and started toward her, holding his hands up to deflect the stream from his face. Jay chortled and darted around the Jeep, then got him again when he looked around at her.

He pushed his wet hair back and his light brown eyes took on that unholy yellow gleam. "You're going to get it now," he said, beginning to grin, and with one bound leaped onto the hood of the Jeep. Jay shrieked and ran to the rear, but the hose caught on the tires as she dragged it after her. She tugged frantically as Steve jumped lightly to the ground. He laughed in a way that made her scream again, and she threw the hose down as she ran for safety.

He grabbed the hose and reversed direction, running back around the front of the Jeep, to free it. He met Jay almost head-on.

"Wait," she said, laughing and begging at the same time as she held up her hand. "It's lunchtime. I came out to tell you. The soup's ready—" A blast of water hit her in the face.

The water was almost unbearably cold. She screamed and tried to run for safety, but he was there every time she turned, and the water soaked her from head to foot. Finally her only means of defense was attack, so she ran straight at him. He was laughing like a maniac, a sound that ceased abruptly when she twisted the nozzle up so the water hit him right in the mouth. They wrestled for control of the nozzle, both of them laughing and yelling as the icy water sprayed all over them.

"Truce, truce!" she yelled, backing away. There was no way she could have gotten any wetter, but then, neither could he. She felt a sense of satisfaction that it had turned out so evenly.

"Are you giving up?" he demanded.

She hooted. "What's to give up? We're both half drowned."

He thought about that and nodded. Then he walked over to the spigot to turn it off and began coiling the hose. "You fight dirty. I like that in a woman."

"That's right, butter me up. You just want to make certain I don't stop cooking."

"The situation being what it is, I'll take anything from you I can get."

Abruptly the humor was gone from the moment. He dropped the hose and straightened, his face hard as he looked at her.

Jay felt her breath catch. He had never been more beautiful to her than he was at that moment, soaking wet, his hair plastered to his skull, badly in need of a shave, and his eyes glittering with masculine intent. Slowly he let his gaze move over her face, then down her body, taking his time as he traced the outline of her form.

Then she realized that he could see more than the outline. The white cotton dress was almost transparent, plastered to her body the way it was. She couldn't stop herself from looking down. Her nipples were hard and erect, plainly visible under the wet cotton, and the fabric was molded to her hips and thighs. With the sun shining through the material, she might as well have been naked for all the protection the dress gave her.

She looked back up at him and froze in place at the look on his face. He was staring at her with such savage male hunger that her heart leaped, making the blood surge through her veins. Her legs trembled as she felt herself begin to grow warm and moist in response, and she inhaled sharply.

His head jerked up. For another moment he was motionless. Her lips were parted slightly, trembling. Her eyes looked heavy. Her nipples were hard little circles plainly visible through the wet dress, her arms limp at her sides as she let him look. He shuddered, and his control snapped.

She couldn't move. He walked toward her without taking his gaze from her, without seeing or hearing anything else, a primal male animal intent on mating. He was breathing hard and deep, his nostrils flaring. Water dripped off him as he moved. She waited, shaking with need and fear, because he was out of control and she knew it. It was an exhilarating terror, freezing her but at the same time filling her with an anticipation so acute she was almost in pain.

Then his hands were on her, and she moaned aloud from the sudden release of tension.

She didn't have time to respond. She had expected to be swept up in his arms and carried to bed, but he had gone far beyond paying attention to niceties. Nothing mattered to him but to have her, right then. He bore her down to the cold, wet earth, which, despite the chinook, still held the long freeze of winter. Jay cried out at the iciness against her back, involuntarily arching upward to escape it. Steve's hard hands pressed her back, and he covered her, his weight pinning her down. He jerked at her dress, pulling the skirt to her waist. "Spread your legs," he said gutturally, though he was already kneeing her thighs apart.

Excitement speared through her. "Yes," she whispered, her hands digging into his shoulders. She wanted him so much that she didn't care where they were or how urgent he was. There would be time for seduction later, as well as worry. Right now there was only this quick, primitive mating.

There was no foreplay, no leisurely petting or stroking. For months there had been too much between them while the final intimacy had been denied, and suddenly the walls were down. He disposed of her panties by the simple means of tearing them apart, then unfastened his pants and shoved them down only as far as was necessary. He pushed her legs wider apart and lowered himself onto her.

She made a little sound of pain as he tried to enter her and couldn't. He swiftly adjusted his position and pushed again, this time sliding deep into her. Shock reverberated through her body as she tried to adjust to his girth, and this time she groaned.

He braced himself on his elbows, and Jay looked up at him dazedly. His yellowish eyes were fierce, his face hard and intent, his neck corded as he drove into her. She arched up to accept him, her heart almost exploding with love. This was what she had wanted, to see his face, to see his eagle-fierce eyes, to imprint his image on her mind and heart even as he imprinted his touch on her body. With the icy earth beneath her and the pure blue sky above, with the bright sun on his face, they were as pure and primitive as their surroundings. No matter what his name or what he did, he was her love, her man.

This was for him. She lifted her hips to meet his thrusts, her flesh quivering under his pounding force. He groaned unintelligibly and slid his arms beneath her to lift her up even more, as if he could grind their bodies so tightly together that they would mesh, then convulsed in release.

She held him tightly, her legs around his hips, her arms about his shoulders as he heaved into her, groaning and shivering. "I love you," she said over and over again, though her lips moved soundlessly and only the warm winds heard her. She closed her eyes, feeling that warm wind on her cheek and his heavy weight both on her and in her, and knew that no matter what happened when he regained his memory, this hard, fast possession had made her his in a way that could never be shattered.

Chapter Ten

They lay together, motionless, the only movement that of the wind stirring their hair, the only sound that of the trees rustling together, sighing. Jay felt dazed by what had just happened, her senses buffeted as if she had just weathered a storm. She was totally incapable of action.

Then he braced his hands and lifted his weight off her, staring down at her with an expression so fierce that she almost cringed from it, without knowing why. He swore, his voice low and gravelly, as he disengaged their bodies and shifted to a kneeling position. Uncertainty paralyzed her as her sluggish mind began trying to grasp the reason for his anger.

He pulled his pants up but didn't bother fastening them; instead he tugged her up and into his arms, lifting her from the ground and rising to his feet with a lithe grace that belied the strength necessary to do it. He climbed the steps and strode into the house without saying a word, then carried her into the bathroom. After carefully standing her on the rug, he bent to turn on the water, then straightened and turned back to her. Her dress was unfastened and gently pulled over her head, leaving her naked and shivering from both chill and reaction. She stood docilely, her arms limp at her sides, her eyes wide and dazed and a little frightened as she watched him. What was *wrong*?

He hurriedly stripped, then lifted her into the tub and stepped in beside her, pulling the shower door closed. Jay moved back, a little bemused by how much room he took up, and watched the rippling muscles in his back as he adjusted the water, then turned on the shower. Warm water blasted out of the shower head, immediately filling the small area with steam. Steve pulled her under the water and held her there even when she gasped a protest, because the water was stinging her cold skin.

"No, you need to get warm," he said roughly, rubbing his hands up and down her arms and shoulders. "Turn around and let me wash your hair."

Numbly she did so, realizing that they must have gotten mud all over them. His hands were gentle as he lathered and rinsed her hair, then washed her all over. She began to feel very warm from the combination of water and the stroking of his soapy hands, first over her breasts and abdomen, then her legs and buttocks, and finally between her legs. Her breathing began to hasten as heat built in her.

His touch slowed, and a spasm twitched his tight facial muscles. Her breathing halted altogether as he probed tantalizingly at the entrance to her body, his fingertips barely stroking, one finger barely entering. She caught at his shoulders, her nails digging into his sleek, wet skin. Her breasts were tight and aching as she hung there in an agony of anticipation, waiting for that small invasion, wanting so much more. She felt him hardening against her hip, and a great shudder of pleasure shook her.

He muttered something, but the sound was so rough she couldn't understand it; then she was in his arms, and his mouth was bruising hers. She yielded to his urgency, sliding her hands to the back of his neck. Their water-slick bodies rubbed together, his abrasive chest hair rasping at her nipples, his muscled stomach rippling against the softness of hers, his hardness pushing at her. "Yes," she whimpered.

"I'm sorry, baby," he said, the words rough and frantic and urgent. He slid his mouth down her throat, biting at the sensitive arch, licking the small hollow at the base, where her pulse throbbed visibly. "I didn't mean to be that rough."

So that was why he was angry, not at her, but at himself. But even that wasn't enough to keep him from having her again. She could feel the hunger in his big, powerful body, and again his loss of control thrilled her in a deeply primitive way. She had been married, but Steve had always kept his cool, kept part of himself securely locked away from her, and the passionate part of her had been hurt, because she'd needed more. The man in her arms now was savage in his hunger, driven out of control by his need for her, and his wildness matched the fierce passion of her own nature. All her life she had needed this answering intensity to balance her; without it, she had withdrawn behind a shell of rigid control, and only now was she being freed.

She clung to him like a vine, her wet body undulating against him. "I love you," she groaned, because that was the only thing she could say, the one outstanding truth in the maze of lies and subterfuges.

He lifted his mouth from her throat, his face so close to hers that his burning gaze was all she could see. "I hurt you," he growled.

She couldn't deny it. "Yes," she said, and fitted her mouth to his, her tongue delicately probing. His arms tightened so convulsively that she couldn't breathe, but breathing didn't matter. Kissing him mattered. Loving him mattered.

But finally he did find some remnant of control, enough to allow him to turn off the water and haul her out of the tub. She never released her hold on his neck as he swept her up and carried her, both of them dripping wet, to his bed. She didn't care about the sheets. All she cared about was his hot mouth on her breasts, the rasp of his slightly roughened fingertips on her silky skin, and finally his powerful invasion of her body. It was still such a shock to her senses that she cried out, instinctively trying to close her thighs. But her legs tightened on his muscled thighs and the movement only drew him deeper.

He ground his teeth together, trying to force himself to stillness when every instinct told him to move. The need was so urgent that it smothered everything else in the world except the woman he held in his arms, the woman whose slim body clasped him so tightly and pushed him to the edge of insanity. But for her sake he managed to hold still until she was more comfortable with him. Lying propped on his elbows so his weight wouldn't crush her, he looked down at her and shuddered with pleasure at the intense, absorbed look on her face as she lifted her hips slightly, tentatively, to accept all of him. A deep groan tore from his chest. He knew he'd been too rough and urgent to allow her time to enjoy it before, but this time she was with him.

Her lips parted slightly in a smile so female it took his breath away, and her deep blue eyes beckoned him, dared him. Once again her hips lifted. "What are you waiting for?" she breathed.

"For you," he answered, and even as he lost himself in the mindless ecstasy of making love to her, the truth of that remained. He'd waited for her forever.

He was a light sleeper, so much so that even in the heavy-limbed aftermath he was disturbed by the damp sheets, a discomfort they hadn't noticed before. Jay lay in his arms, exhausted and deeply asleep; he didn't want to disturb her, but neither did he want her to become chilled from the wetness. He eased from the bed and lifted her light weight in his arms, then carried her into the other bedroom to place her on the dry bed. She made a disgruntled noise as he jostled her, then relaxed again, and her breathing evened out as he stroked her back. He joined her on the bed, and she snuggled closer, into his hard, possessive embrace.

The way he felt about her was so intense it edged into pain. Even without his memory, he knew no other woman had ever shattered his control as she did. He'd never desired another woman so intensely, never would have waited as long as he'd waited for her. She overshadowed every other concern. Because of her, he hadn't dwelled on his loss of memory, beyond a peculiar irritation and a certain detached interest in the curiosities of what he had retained. His past life didn't matter, because Jay was here in the present. They were linked in a way that went beyond memory.

A slight frown creased his brow as he held her, his rough hand sliding from the curve of her hip to the warmly resilient mound of her breast. Of all the knowledge he'd kept, why wasn't any of it of Jay? Those were the memories he resented losing. He wanted to remember every minute he'd spent with her, and he wanted to remember why he'd let her slip away from him. He wanted to remember their wedding, the first time he'd made love to her, and the total lack of those memories ate at him. She was the core of his life; why hadn't *something* been familiar? Why hadn't he felt some deep-seated recognition of the silkiness of her skin, the rounded curves of her high breasts or the rose-brown of her small nipples? Why hadn't there been some sense of familiarity in the tight sheath of her body as he entered her?

But everything had been new.

She moved slightly against him, and he stilled his stroking hand, content to simply hold her. They would be married as soon as he could talk her into it, and now he had a very powerful weapon at his disposal.

The scene exploded in his mind. There was a laughing bride and a groom looking excited, proud, wary and impatient all at once. The groom shook his head, beaming, and the bride hugged him tightly. "You made it!" she said exultantly. "I knew you would!"

An older woman and man hugged him just as tightly. "I'm glad you're back, son," the man said, and the woman cried a little even as she smiled at him, the smile full of love. Then there was a rush of other people to shake his hand and hug him and clap him on the back, and the scene dissolved in a confusion of voices.

He lay rigidly, his jaw clenched with the effort required not to jackknife out of bed. Where in hell had *that* memory come from? The man had called him "son," but that could as easily have been a title of affection as one denoting a relationship. He didn't have a family, so they must have been close friends, but Jay had said he'd always been a loner. Who were they? Did they worry about him? Did Jay know anything about them?

Hell, was it even something that had really happened, or a scene from a movie he'd watched?

Movie. Just thinking the word triggered another flashback, but this one was complete with rolling credits. It was a television special on Afghanistan. Then it became another movie, starring a widely acclaimed actor. It was a good movie. Then, in slow motion, the scene shifted. He was standing on a rooftop with the same actor when the man pulled a .45 automatic and pointed it at him. Serious business, a .45. It could have a major impact on a man's future. But the guy was too close, and too rattled. Steve saw himself lash out with his foot, sending the gun flying. The actor staggered back and tripped, fell over the low wall and screamed as he dropped the full seven stories to the ground.

Steve stared at the bedroom ceiling, feeling sweat run down his ribs. Was that another movie? Of all the things he could remember, why a series of films? And why were they so realistic, as if he had stepped into the action? He'd have to ask the doctor about that, but at least it was a sign his memory was returning, just as they'd told him it probably would. He needed to make the trip anyway, to have his eyes checked; it was a real strain to read, and the strain hadn't lessened. He definitely needed glasses. Glasses...

An elderly man smiled benignly at him and removed his glasses, placing them on the desk. "Congratulations, Mr. Stone," he said.

He stifled a curse as the scene faded. This was weird; why would that old guy call him "Mr. Stone" unless he'd been using an assumed name? Yeah, that made sense, unless it was just another scene out of another movie. It could just be something he'd watched rather than something that had actually happened.

Jay stirred in his arms and abruptly woke, lifting her head to stare at him in alarm. "What's wrong?"

She had sensed his tension, just as she had from the beginning. He managed a smile and touched her cheek with the backs of his fingers, a different kind of tension taking over his muscles. "Nothing," he assured her. She looked sleepy and sensual, her eyes heavy-lidded, her luscious mouth swollen from contact with his firmer lips.

She looked around. "We're in my room," she said in bewilderment.

"Mmm. The sheets on my bed were wet, so I brought you in here."

Warm color tinted her cheeks as she thought of how the sheets had gotten so wet, but her smile was both secret and content. She lifted her hand and touched his face, much as he had touched hers; her dark blue eyes drifted over his features with aching tenderness, examining each line and plane, feeding the need in her heart. She was unaware of her expression, but he saw it, and his chest constricted. He wanted to say, "Don't love me like that," but he didn't, because it was essential to him that she love him exactly like that.

He cleared his throat. "We have a choice."

"We do? Of course we do. Of what?"

"We can get up and eat the lunch you were cooking—" he broke off to lift his head and look at the clock

"—three hours ago, or we can try to wreck this bed, too."

She considered it. "I think we'd better have lunch, or I won't have the energy to help you wreck the bed."

"Good thinking." He hugged her, reluctant to get up despite his own hunger, and found his hands stroking down her sides in sensual enjoyment. Then he paused and moved his hand around to her stomach. "Unless you want to get married this weekend, we'd better do something about birth control."

Jay's heart felt as if it had abruptly swollen so large that it filled her entire chest. For a few glorious hours she'd forgotten how hemmed in she was by this tortuous maze of deception. She wanted nothing more than to simply say "Yes, let's get married," but she didn't dare. Not until he knew who he was—and *she* knew who he was—and he still said he wanted to marry her. So she ignored the first part of his statement and merely answered the second. "We don't have to worry about birth control. I'm on the Pill. My doctor put me on it seven months ago, because my periods had gotten so erratic."

His eyes narrowed a little and his hand lay heavier on her stomach. "Is something wrong?"

"No. It was just stress from my job. I could probably do without them now." Then she smiled and turned her face into his shoulder. "Except for a sudden development."

He grunted. "Sudden, hell. I've been hard for two months. But we could still get married this weekend."

She eased out of his embrace and got up, her face troubled as she put on fresh underwear and got a sweater from the closet, pulling it over her head.

He watched her from the bed. His voice was very soft and raspy when he spoke. "I want an answer."

Harried, she pushed her tangled hair out of her eyes. "Steve—" She stopped, almost cringing at the necessity of calling him by that name. Now more than ever, she wanted, needed, to know her lover's name. "I can't marry you until you've gotten your memory back."

He threw the sheet back and stood, magnificently naked. Jay's pulse rate skittered as she looked at him. All the miles he'd run and the wood he'd chopped had corded his body with muscles. He didn't look as if he'd ever been injured, except for his scars. Her heart settled into a slow, heavy beat. She had cradled his weight, taken his pounding invasion, returned his fire with her own. As tender as she felt now in different parts of her body, she could still feel herself grow warm and liquid as she looked at him.

"What difference does my memory make?" he snapped, and she jerked her gaze upward, realizing that he was angry. "No other woman has a claim on me, and you know it, so don't bring up that crap again. Why should we wait?"

"I want you to be certain," she said, her voice troubled.

"Damn it, I am certain!"

"How can you be, when you don't know what's happened? I just don't want you to regret marrying me when everything comes back to you." She tried a smile, and it only wobbled a little. "We're together, and we have time. That will have to be enough for now."

Steve forced himself to be content with that, and in many ways it was enough. They lived together in the truest sense of the word, as partners, friends and lovers. It was a week before the snows came again, and in that week they explored every inch of their high meadow. He showed her the laser-beam sensor he'd installed across the trail and demonstrated how to operate both the radio and the computer. It was a relief not to have to hide from her how deeply he'd been involved in espionage, though she got a little huffy with him because all the equipment had been hidden from her in the shed and only now had he gotten around to telling her about it.

He liked making her lose her temper. It was exciting, in a primitive way, to watch those blue eyes narrow like a cat's. It was the final sign that he'd tormented her into attack. The day he'd thought she was an intruder and tracked her in the snow, then tackled her, her rage had startled him, caught him off balance, but it had excited him. Most people who knew Jay would never think she was capable of that kind of anger, or that she would physically fight anyone. It told him a lot about her, about the passionate, volatile side of her personality and about what it took to bring it out. Probably very few people could make her angry, but because she loved him, he could. And after he'd provoked her to anger, he liked to wrestle with her and love her out of her temper.

Physically she delighted him. She was still too thin, though she ate well, but he liked to watch her trim hips and rounded buttocks in her tight jeans too much to complain. Her skin was satiny, her breasts high and round, her exotic mouth full and pouty; no matter how she dressed, she turned him on because he knew what lay under those clothes. He also knew that all he had to do was reach for her and she'd turn into his arms, warm and willing. That kind of response enchanted him; there was something so new about it, as if he'd never known it before.

Then one morning they got up to find that it had snowed again during the night, and it continued snowing all during the day, not hard, just a continuous veil of flakes sifting down over the meadow. Except for trips outside to bring in more firewood, Jay and Steve spent the day in the cabin, watching old movies. That was an extra benefit of the satellite dish; they could always find something interesting to watch on television, if they were in the mood. It was perfectly suited to a lazy day when they had nothing better to do than to lie around and watch the fat snowflakes drifting down.

Just before dark, Steve left to check the area, something he always did. While he was gone Jay began cooking dinner, humming as she did so, because she was so contented. This was paradise. She knew it couldn't last; when his memory returned, even if he still wanted to marry her, their lives would change. They would leave here, find another home. She would have to find another job. Other things would take up their time. This was time set aside, out of the real world, but she meant to enjoy every minute of it. Briefly a dark thought intruded: This could be all she had. Perhaps it was. If so, these days were all the more precious.

Steve entered through the back door, slapping snow off his shoulders and shaking it out of his hair before taking off his thick coat. "Nothing but rabbit tracks." He looked thoughtful. "Do you like rabbit?"

Jay turned from the cheese she was grating for the spaghetti. "If you shoot the Easter Bunny..." she began in a threatening tone.

"It was just a question," he said, and grabbed her for a kiss, then rubbed his cold, beard-roughened cheek against hers. "You smell good. Like onion and garlic and tomato sauce." Actually, she smelled like herself, that sweet, warm, womanly scent he associated with her and no one else. He buried his cold nose against her neck and inhaled it, feeling the familiar tension growing in his loins.

"You won't get any points for telling me I smell like onions and garlic," she said, returning to her chore even though he kept his arms looped around her waist.

"Even if I tell you how crazy I am about onions and garlic?"

"Humph. You're like all men. You'll say anything when you're hungry."

Chuckling, he released her to set the table and begin buttering the rolls. "How would you like to take a trip?"

"I'd love to see Hawaii."

"I was thinking more in terms of Colorado Springs. Or maybe Denver."

"I've *been* to Colorado Springs," she said, then looked at him curiously over her shoulder. "Why are we going to Colorado Springs?"

"I'm assuming Frank doesn't want us returning to Washington, even briefly, so he'll fly the doctor out to check my eyes. That means, logically, either Colorado Springs or Denver, and I'm betting Colorado Springs. I'm also betting he doesn't want the doctor to know the location of the cabin, so that means we go to him."

She had known he would have to have his eyes checked again, but just talking about it brought the real world intruding into their private paradise. It would feel strange even seeing other people, much less talking to them. But reading strained his eyes, and enough time had passed for them to realize his sight wasn't going to improve. She thought of how he would look in glasses, and a warm feeling began spreading in her stomach. Sexy. She gave him a smile. "Yeah, I think I'd like to make a trip. I've been eating my own cooking for a long time now."

"I'll get in touch with Frank after dinner." He could have done it then, but filling his stomach was more important. Jay made great spaghetti, and getting in touch with Frank could be time-consuming. First things first.

After the dinner dishes had been cleaned and Steve was in the shed contacting Frank, Jay stretched out on the rug in front of the fire, for the first time thinking about the chic little apartment in New York that Frank had been keeping for her. It contrasted sharply with the rustic comfort of the cabin, but she much preferred the cabin. She would hate to leave it; it would be beautiful here during the summer, but she wondered how much longer they would be here. Surely Steve's memory would return before then, and even if it didn't, how much longer would it be before Frank told him the truth? They couldn't let him live another man's life forever. Or could they? Had that been the plan? Did they somehow know he'd never get his memory back?

The mirrors kept reflecting back different answers, different facets to the puzzle, different solutions. And none of them fit.

"Are you asleep?" he asked softly.

She gasped and rolled over, her heart jumping. "I didn't hear you come in. You didn't make any noise." He always moved silently, like a cat, but she should have heard the back door. She'd been so deep in thought that the sounds hadn't registered.

"The better to sneak up on you, my dear," he growled in his best big-bad-wolf voice. He joined her on the rug, sinking his hands into her hair as he angled her mouth up toward his. He kissed her slowly, deeply, taking his time and using his tongue. Her breathing altered, and her eyes grew heavy lidded. Desire was a heavy warmth inside her, slowly expanding until it completely filled her.

They weren't in any hurry. It felt too good to lie there in the warmth of the crackling fire and savor their kisses. But eventually the heat was too much, and she moaned as he unbuttoned her flannel shirt, parting the edges to press his lips to the swollen curves of her breasts. He lay on top of her, his heavy legs controlling hers even though she twisted restlessly. She wanted more. Moaning again, her voice sharp with need, she turned until her nipple brushed against his mouth. Lazily he extended his tongue and licked it, then clamped his mouth over it and sucked strongly, giving her what she needed.

The firelight burnished her hair with golden lights and her skin with a rosy glow as he unfastened her jeans and pulled them off. Her mouth was red and moist, glistening with the sheen of his kisses. Abruptly he couldn't wait any longer and jerked his own clothes off. The flannel shirt still hung around her shoulders, but even that was too much. He pulled it away from her and knelt between her legs, draping her thighs over his as he bent forward to enter her, fusing their bodies as surely as their lives were fused.

They lay together for a long time afterward, too content to move. He put another log on the fire and pulled on his jeans, then put his own shirt around her to stave off any chill. She sat in the circle of his arms, her head on his shoulder, wishing nothing would ever happen to disturb this happiness.

He watched the waving yellow flames, his rough chin rubbing back and forth against her hair. "Do you want kids?" he asked absently.

The question startled her enough that she lifted her head from his shoulder. "I...think I do." she replied. "I've never really thought about it, because it just didn't seem like an option, but now..." Her voice trailed off.

"Before, we didn't have much of a marriage. I don't want it to be like that again. I want to come home every night, live a normal life." He tightened his arms around her. "I'd like to have a couple of kids, but that's a mutual decision. I didn't know how you felt about it."

"I like kids," she said softly, but guilt assailed her. They hadn't had *any* kind of a marriage before! He was feeling guilty for another man's acts.

"Yeah, I like them, too." He smiled, still watching the fire. "I get a kick out of watching Amy—"

Jay jerked away from him, her eyes wide with something like panic in them. "Who's Amy?"

Steve's face was hard, his mouth grim. "I don't know," he muttered. "I feel as if I just ran into a brick wall. The words just slipped out, then *bam*! I hit the wall and there's nothing."

Jay felt sick. Had she been so wrong in trusting that Frank wouldn't have set this up if Steve had been married? Was he a father as well as a husband?

Steve was watching her and sensed the direction of her thoughts, if not the content. "No, I'm not married and I don't have any kids," he said sharply, pulling her back to him. "It's probably just a friend's little girl. Do you know anyone with a little girl named Amy?"

She shook her head, not looking at him. The terror was back; she felt stiff with it. Was his memory returning? When it did, would he leave? Paradise could end at any time.

Steve lay awake long after they had gone to bed that night. Jay slept in his arms, as she had every night since the chinook blew, her hair streaming over his left shoulder and her warm breath sighing against his neck. Her bare, silky body was pressed all along his left side, and her slender arm was draped across his chest. She had looked so panicked for a second when he'd mentioned Amy's name, whoever Amy was. He held her closer, trying to erase that panic even from her sleep.

This would probably happen a lot, a casual remark triggering flashes of memory. He hoped they wouldn't all scare her so much. Was she truly afraid he wouldn't want her when his memory returned? God, couldn't she feel how much he loved her? It went beyond memory. It was in his bones, buried in the very depths of his existence.

Amy. *Amy.*

The name flashed through his mind like fire and suddenly he saw a little girl with glossy dark hair, giggling as she shoved a chubby, dimpled fist into her mouth. *Amy.*

His heart began pounding. His memory had actually supplied a face to go with the name. He didn't know who she was, but he knew her name, and now her face. The mental picture faded, but he concentrated and found he could recall it, just like a real memory. Just as he'd told Jay, she must be a friend's daughter, someone he'd met since their divorce.

He relaxed, pleased that the memory had solidified. His sexual satisfaction made his body feel heavy and boneless, and his chest began to rise and fall in the deeper rhythm of sleep.

"Unca Luke, Unca Luke!"

The childish voices echoed in his head and the movie began to unwind in his mind. Two kids. Two boys, tearing across a green lawn, jumping and shrieking "Unca Luke" at the tops of their lungs as they ran.

Another scene. Northern Ireland. Belfast. He recognized it even as a tingle of dread ran up his spine. Two little boys played in the street, then suddenly looked up, hesitated and ran.

Flash. One of the first two little boys looked up with a wobbly lower lip and tears in his eyes and said, "Please, Unca Dan."

Flash. Dan Rather stacked papers at his newsdesk while the credits rolled.

Flash. A bumper sticker on a station wagon said, I'd Rather Be at Disney World.

Mickey Mouse dancing... Flash... a mouse crawling through the garbage in an alley... Flash... a grenade sailing in slow motion through the air and hitting a garbage can with a loud thump; then a louder thump and the can goes sailing... Flash... a white sailboat with sassy red-and-white striped sails tacking closer to shore and a tanned young man waves... Flash flash flash...

The scenes ripped through his consciousness, and they were truly only flashes, following each other like pages of a book being flipped through in front of his eyes.

He was sweating again. Damn, these free-association memories were hell. What did they mean? Had they truly happened? He wouldn't mind them if he could tell which ones were real and which ones were just something he'd seen on television or in a movie, or maybe even imagined from a scene in a book. Okay, some of them were obvious, like the one of Dan Rather with the credits rolling across his face. But he'd watched network news many times since the bandages had come off his eyes, so that could even be a recent memory.

But... Uncle Luke. Uncle Dan. Something about those kids, and those names, seemed very real, just as Amy was real.

He eased out of bed, being very careful not to wake Jay, and walked into the living room where he stood for a long time in front of the banked fire, watching the embers glow. Full memory was close, and he knew it. It was as if all he had to do was turn a corner and everything would be there; but turning that mental corner wasn't as easy as it sounded. He had become a different man in the months since the explosion; he was trying to connect two separate people and merge them into one.

He had been absently rubbing his fingertips with his thumb. When he noticed what he was doing, he lifted his hand to look at it. The calluses were back, courtesy of chopping wood, but his fingertips were still smooth. How much of him was left, or had his identity been erased as surely as his fingerprints had been? When he looked in the mirror, how much of it was Steve Crossfield and how much of it was courtesy of the reconstructive surgery? His face was changed, his voice was changed, his fingerprints gone.

He was new. He had been born out of the darkness, brought to life by Jay's voice calling him toward the light.

Regardless of what he did or didn't remember, he still had Jay. She was a part of him that surgery couldn't change.

The room had taken on a chill as the fire died, and finally he felt the coldness on his naked body. He returned to the bedroom and slipped under the quilt, feeling Jay's body warmth wrap around him. She murmured something, moving closer to him in her sleep, seeking her usual position.

Instantly desire fired through him, as urgent as if it hadn't been slaked only an hour or so before. "Jay," he said, his voice low and dark, and he pulled her beneath him. She woke and reached for him, her hands sliding around his neck, and in the darkness they loved each other until he had no room for memories other than those they made together.

Chapter Eleven

They left the cabin early the next morning so they could rendezvous with Frank at Colorado Springs that afternoon. Jay felt a wrench at leaving the cabin; it had been their private world for so long that, away from it, she felt exposed. Only the thought that they would be returning the next day gave her the courage to leave it at all. She knew that eventually she would have to leave it forever, but she wasn't ready to face that day right now. She wanted more time with the man she loved.

She intended to ask Frank the name of the American agent who had been "killed." He might not tell her, but she had to ask. Even if she couldn't say it aloud, she needed to know, she had to put a name to her love. She looked at him as he skillfully handled the Jeep, holding it steady even on the snow, and her heart swelled. He was big and rough-looking, not handsome at all with his rearranged features, but just one glance from those fierce yellowish eyes had the power to make her dizzy with delight. How could they ever have thought they could pass this man off as Steve Crossfield?

Their subterfuge was riddled with holes, but she hadn't seen them until she had been too deeply in love with him to care. They had relied on shock and urgency to keep her from asking the pointed questions to which they would have had no answers, such as why they didn't use blood type or their own agent's dental records to determine the identity of the patient. She had known at the time that Frank was hiding something from her, but she had been too concerned over "Steve" to think it was anything more than protecting the details of a classified mission. The truth was that she had been misled so easily because she had wanted to be; after the first time she had seen him lying in the hospital, so desperately wounded but still fighting with that grim determination of his that burned through unconsciousness, she had wanted nothing more than to be by his side and help him fight.

They were to stay at a different motel than the one they'd been in before, because Frank didn't want to take the chance the desk clerk might recognize them. They even used different names. When they got there, Frank had already arrived, and he'd made reservations for them under the names of Michael Carter and Faye Wheeler. Separate rooms. Steve looked distinctly displeased, but placed Jay's overnighter in her room without comment and went along to his own room. The eye specialist checked Steve's eyes immediately; then he was taken to an optometrist to be fitted for glasses, which would be ready for him the next morning. Jay remained behind, wondering what strings Frank had pulled and whose arms he had twisted to get everything done so fast.

They returned a little after dark, and Steve came immediately to Jay's room. "Hi, baby," he said, stepping inside and closing the door behind him. Before she could answer he was kissing her, his hands tight on her arms, his mouth hard and searching.

She shivered with excitement, crowding closer to his body as she dug her fingers into his cold hair. He smelled like wind and snow, and his skin was cold, but his tongue was warm and probing. Finally he lifted his head, a very male look of satisfaction stamped on his hard face. He rubbed his thumb across her lips, which were reddened from contact with his. "Sweetheart, I may freeze my naked butt off sneaking into your room tonight, but I'm *not* sleeping alone."

"I have a suggestion," she purred.

"Let's hear it."

"Leave your clothes on until you get here."

He laughed and kissed her again. Her mouth was driving him crazy; it had the most erotic effect on him. Kissing her was more arousing than actually making love had been with other women—and just for a moment, before they faded away, some of those other women were in his mind.

"The doctor is already on his way back to Washington. Frank is staying until the morning, so it's the three of us again. Are you hungry? Frank's stomach is still on Washington time."

"Actually, I am a little hungry. We don't keep late hours ourselves, you know."

He looked at the bed. "I know."

Jay hoped to have the chance to ask Frank about the agent's name; she couldn't take the risk of asking him in Steve's presence, because the sound of his own name might trigger his memory, and she couldn't face the possibility of that. She wanted him to remember, but she wanted it to be when they were alone in their high meadow. If the chance to talk to Frank didn't present itself, she could always call him after they'd retired to their individual rooms for the night, provided Steve didn't come straight to hers, but she didn't think he would. He'd probably take a shower first, and put on fresh clothes. She sighed, weary of having to second-guess and predict; she wasn't cut out for this business.

Steve noted the sigh, and the faint desperation in her eyes. She hadn't said anything, but that look had been there since he'd had that first flash of memory the day before. It puzzled him; he couldn't think of any reason why Jay should dread his returning memory. Because it puzzled him and because there was no logical reason, he couldn't let it go. It wasn't in his makeup. When something bothered him, he worried at it until it made sense. He never quit, never let go. His sister had often said he was at least half bulldog—   Sister?

He was quiet as the three of them ate dinner at an Italian restaurant. Part of him enjoyed the spicy food, and part of him was actively involved in the easy conversation around the table, but another part of him examined the sliver of memory from every angle. If he had a sister, why had he told Jay he was an orphan? Why hadn't Frank had a record of any relatives? That was the screwy part. He could accept that he might have told Jay a different version of his life, because he didn't know what the circumstances had been at the time, but it was impossible that Frank hadn't had a list of next of kin. That was assuming he was remembering "real" things.

A sister. His logic told him it was impossible. His guts told him his logic could take a flyer. A sister. Amy. *Unca Luke! Unca Luke!* The childish voices reverberated in his head even as he laughed at something Frank said. *Unca Dan.* Unca Luke. Unca Luke Unca Luke...Luke...Luke...

"Are you all right?" Jay asked, her eyes dark with concern as she put her hand lightly on his wrist. She could feel tension emanating from him and was vaguely startled that Frank hadn't seemed to notice anything unusual.

The pounding left his head as he looked at her and smiled. He'd gladly count his past well lost as long as he could have Jay. The sensory umbilical cord linking them was as acutely sensitive as the strings on a precisely tuned Stradivarius. "It's just a headache," he said. "The drive was a strain on my eyes." Both statements were true, though the second wasn't the cause of the first. Also, there hadn't been that much strain. His problem was the precise, close-up focusing needed for reading; his distance vision was as sharp as ever, which was better than twenty-twenty. He had the vision of a jet pilot.

Jay returned to her conversation with Frank, but she was as aware of Steve's fading tension as she had been of the fact that he'd been as taut as a guide wire. Had something happened that afternoon that he hadn't told her? A feeling of dread almost overwhelmed her, and she wanted badly to be back at the cabin.

When they returned to the motel, she noted with relief that Steve went to his own room rather than stopping to talk with Frank or immediately following her to hers. She darted to the phone and dialed Frank's room. He answered on the first ring.

"It's Jay." She identified herself.

"Is something wrong?" He was immediately alert.

"No, everything's okay. It's just that something's been bothering me, but I didn't want to ask you in front of Steve."

In his room, Frank tensed. Had they failed to cover all bases? "Is it about Steve?"

"Well, no, not really. The agent who died . . . what was his name? It's been on my mind a lot lately, that he died and I never even heard his name."

"There's no reason you should have. You'd never met him."

"I know," she said softly. "I just wanted to know something about him. It could have been Steve. Now that he's dead, there's no reason to keep his name secret, is there?"

Frank thought. He could give her a fictitious name, but he decided to tell her at least that much of the truth. She'd know his name eventually, and it might help if she could simply think a mistake had been made. It would give her a small fact she could focus on for reference. "His name was Lucas Stone."

"Lucas Stone." Her voice was very soft as she repeated the name. "Was he married? Did he have a family?"

"No, he wasn't married." He deliberately didn't answer her second question.

"Thanks for telling me. It's bothered me that I didn't know." He'd never know how much, she thought as she quietly replaced the receiver. Lucas Stone. She repeated the name over and over in her mind, applying it to a battered face and feeling her heart begin to pound. Lucas Stone. Yes.

Only then did she realize what a mistake she'd made. If it had been difficult before to refer to him as Steve, it would be almost impossible now. Steve had been a stolen name, but one she'd used because there had been no alternative. What if the name Lucas slipped out?

She sat on the bed for a long time while she mentally flailed against the hall of mirrors that trapped her with its false reflections. The things she didn't know bound her as securely as the things she knew, until she was afraid to trust her own instincts. She wasn't made for deception; she was straightforward, which was one reason why she hadn't fitted into the world of investment banking, a world that required a certain measure of "slickery," that balance of slickness and trickery.

Finally, too tired to open any more blank doors, she took a shower and got ready for bed. When she came out of the bathroom, Lucas—*Steve*! she reminded herself frantically—was stretched out on the bed, already partially undressed.

She looked at the locked door. "Haven't we done this before?"

He rolled to his feet and caught her arms, pulling her to him. "With one difference. A big difference."

He smelled of soap and shaving cream, and the underlying muskiness of man. She clung to him, pressing her face into his neck to inhale that special scent. What would she do if he left her? It would be a life without color, forever incomplete. Slowly she ran her hands over his broad chest, rubbing her fingers through the crisp, curly hair and feeling the warmth of his skin, then the iron layer of muscles beneath. He was so hard that her fingers barely made an impression. Bemused, she pressed experimentally on his upper arm, watching as her fingernails turned white from the pressure but had noticeably little effect on him.

"What are you doing?" he asked curiously.

"Seeing how hard you are."

"Honey, that's not the right place."

Her face was bright with laughter as she swiftly looked up at him. "I think I know all your other places."

"Is that so? There are places, and then there are places. Some places need a lot more attention than others." As he spoke he began moving her toward the bed. He was already aroused, his hardness pressing against her. Jay moved her hand down to cover the ridge beneath his jeans.

"Is this one of the places in need of attention?"

"A lot of attention," he assured her as he levered them both onto the bed. He felt her legs move, her hips lifting to cradle him, and all amusement faded out of his eyes, leaving them fierce and narrow. It was a look that made Jay shudder in exquisite anticipation.

She looked up at him, her face soft and shining as his hands began moving tenderly on her body. "I love you," she said, and her heart echoed, *Lucas*.

It was different the next morning, as if the world had altered during the night, but he couldn't quite put his finger on the difference. It was an oddly familiar feeling, as if he were more at home with himself. Jay was in his arms, her sleek, golden-brown hair lying tangled on his shoulder. If they had been in the cabin he would have got up to rebuild the fire, then returned to bed for some early-morning loving. Instead he had to go to his own room to shave and dress. That damn Frank. He'd booked separate rooms knowing they needed only one. But Jay wasn't like all the other women; Jay was special, and maybe this was Frank's tribute to her specialness.

Other women. The thought nagged at him after he left Jay and returned to his own room in the biting cold of dawn. His memory was returning, not in one big, melodramatic rush, like a light switch being turned on, but in unconnected bits and pieces. Faces and names were surfacing. Instead of feeling elated, however, he was aware of a growing sense of caution. He hadn't told Frank his memory was coming back; he'd wait until it had truly returned and he'd had time to consider the situation. Wariness was second nature to him, just as he automatically checked his room to make certain no one had entered it in his absence.

He showered and shaved, but as he shaved he found himself staring at his face in the mirror, trying to find his past in the reflection. How could he recognize himself when his face had been changed? What had he looked like before? He wondered if Jay had a picture of him; it would be an old one, if she'd kept any at all. But women tended to keep mementos and their divorce hadn't been a bitter one, so maybe she hadn't destroyed whatever pictures she'd had. Maybe seeing one would give him a link to the past.

Hell, why should it? He stared at himself in disgust. He hadn't recognized Jay or Frank; why should he recognize his old face? The face he knew was the face he could see now, and it wouldn't win any prizes.

He looked as if he'd played too many football games without a helmet.

Still, the sensation lingered that he was on the brink of... something. It was there, just beyond his reach.

It nagged at him in little ways, like the ease with which he slipped his shoulder holster on, and the familiarity of the gun in his hand as he checked it, then slid it into place. The ease and familiarity had been there before, but now they were somehow different, as if the link between past and present were returning. Soon. It would happen soon.

The day was uneventful, but the feeling of anticipation didn't leave him. They all met to eat breakfast; then he and Frank drove to the optical lab and picked up his glasses. On the way back he asked, "Have you found this Piggot guy yet?"

"Not yet. He surfaced a month ago, but he went underground again before we could get to him."

"Is he good?"

Frank hesitated. "Damn good. One of the best. His psychological profile says he's a psychopath, but very controlled, very professional. His jobs are a matter of pride to him. That's why he wants you. You screwed him up the way no one else ever had. You spoiled his job, killed his 'employees' and managed to hit him hard enough that he had to go underground for months to recover."

"I may have hit him hard, but it wasn't hard enough," Steve said remotely. "Do you have a picture of him?"

"Not with me. There's only one. We got him with a telescopic lens, and it's grainy. He's about five-ten, a hundred and forty-five pounds, blond, forty-two years old. His left earlobe is missing, also courtesy of you. His reputation suffered."

"Yeah, well, some days I'm a little cranky."

That was vintage Lucas Stone. Frank felt the shock of it like a slap, but he kept his hands steady on the wheel. "Is your memory coming back?"

"Not yet," Steve lied. He could see Geoffrey Piggot, whiplash thin, malignant, cold. Another face to go with a name.

He was very quiet on the drive back to the cabin. Jay glanced at him, but sunglasses hid his eyes, and she could read nothing in his expression. She still sensed the tension in him, just as she had the night before, during dinner. "Do you have another headache?" she finally asked.

"No." Then he softened the bluntness of his answer by reaching over to rub the backs of his fingers against her jaw. "I feel okay."

"Did Frank say anything that's bothering you?"

Briefly he considered the disadvantages of letting someone get so close to you that they could read your moods, but then he counted that battle well lost in Jay's case, because as far as he was concerned, she couldn't get close enough to suit him. And he hadn't *let* her get close; it had simply happened.

"No. He told me a few things about the guy who tried to make me into beef stew—"

"Oh, gross!" she said, slapping his hand away, and he laughed at her.

"I was just thinking about him, that's all."

After a moment she curled up in the seat and rested her head against the back. "I'll be glad to get home."

He was in total agreement with that. They had been alone together for so long that this trip had almost brought on culture shock. Neon lights and traffic were a definite jolt to a system that was used to fir trees, snow and a deep, deep silence. Right now he would welcome a trip to civilization only if he and Jay were getting blood tests and a marriage license.

Blood tests.

Suddenly he felt alert, just as he'd felt a thousand times before when his life hung in the balance. Adrenaline spurted into his veins, and his heart began racing, but not as fast as his brain. A blood test. Damn it, it didn't fit. Why had they needed Jay to identify him when they had all the means at hand? He was their agent. Granted, his fingerprints were gone, he'd been unconscious and his voice damaged, but they still had his blood type and dental records. It should have been easy enough to establish his identity. It followed, then, that they hadn't needed Jay at all, but had definitely wanted her for some reason.

He went over what Jay had told him. They had wanted her to identity him because they couldn't make a positive ID, and they'd needed to know if their agent had bought the farm, because Steve and this other guy had been caught in the explosion and one of them was dead. That meant there must have been two agents on location, but it wouldn't have changed the fact that Frank had the means at hand to identify both of them. Supposedly he and this other agent had physically resembled each other, about the same height and weight, and with the same coloring. There still wasn't any problem with identification, even if he stretched coincidence and allowed that they both might have had the same blood type. That still left dental records.

Damn, he felt like a fool. Why hadn't he seen this before? They had wanted Jay in this for some reason, but identification hadn't been it. What kind of scheme was Frank running?

Think. He had to think. He felt as if he were trying to put a puzzle together without all the pieces, so no matter how he moved things around they still didn't fit. If he could just remember, damn it!

Why would Frank lie to Jay? Why concoct the story that he and the other agent so closely resembled each other? Why insist that he needed her at all?

Why did they need Jay?

Voices tumbled in on him. *"Congratulations, Mr. Stone"*... *"I'm glad you're back, son"*... *"Unca Luke! Unca Luke!"* Stone...son...Unca Luke... son...Luke...Stone...

Luke Stone.

His hands jerked on the steering wheel. He felt as if he'd been hit in the chest. Luke Stone. Lucas Stone. *Damn Frank Payne to hell! His name was Lucas Stone!*

As soon as he'd turned that mental corner, all the memories came rushing at him in a confusing flood, filling his mind with so much clatter that he could barely drive. He didn't dare stop, didn't dare let Jay know what he was feeling. He felt... God, he didn't know how he felt. Battered. His head hurt, but at the same time he was aware of an enormous sense of relief. He had his identity back, his sense of self. Finally he knew himself.

He was Lucas Stone. He had a family and friends, a past.

But he wasn't Jay's ex-husband. He wasn't Steve Crossfield. He wasn't the man she thought she was in love with.

So that was why she'd been brought in. There had been only one agent at the explosion, and he was that man. Steve Crossfield must have been there for some reason, and he had died there. Lucas tried to form his memories of the meeting, but they were blurred, fragmented. They would probably never come back. But he did remember seeing a tall, lean man walking up the street, his outline reflected on the wet pavement under the streetlight. That could have been Steve Crossfield. He didn't remember anything after that, though now he was remembering making contact, setting up the meeting with Minyard, going to the meeting site. He'd looked up, seen the man...then nothing. Everything after that was a blank, until Jay's voice had pulled him out of the darkness.

His cover had been blown, obviously. Piggot was after him; that was the reason for the charade. Pulling Jay in, duping her into thinking he was her ex-husband, having him positively identified as Steve Crossfield, was the best cover the Man could concoct for him until they could neutralize Piggot. The Man never underestimated his enemies, and Piggot was, as Frank had said, very good. The extent of the Man's deception also told Lucas that the Man suspected there was a mole in his ranks and hadn't trusted regular channels.

So they'd "buried" him, and he'd awakened to another name, another face, another life, even another man's wife.

No, damn it! Savagery filled him, and his knuckles turned white as he automatically negotiated the icy patches on the road. Maybe he wasn't Steve Cross-field, but Jay was his. *His.* Lucas Stone's woman.

Silently and at length, he cursed the Man and Frank for everything he could think of, ranging back over several generations of their ancestors. Not Frank so much, because he could see the Man's fine hand in this. Nobody had a mind as intricate as Kell Sabin's; that was how he'd gotten to be the Man. They had probably—no, almost certainly—saved his life, assuming there was a mole passing information to Piggot, but they weren't the ones who had to tell Jay he wasn't her ex-husband. They didn't have to tell her that the man she loved was dead and she'd been sleeping with a stranger.

What would she say? More important, what would she do?

He couldn't lose her. He could stand anything except that. He expected, and could handle, shock, anger, even fear, but he couldn't stand it if she looked at him with hate in those deep blue eyes. He couldn't let her walk away from him.

Immediately he began examining the situation from all angles, looking for a solution, but even as he looked, he knew there wasn't one. He couldn't marry her using Crossfield's name, because such a marriage wouldn't be legal, and besides, he'd be damned if he'd let her carry another man's name. He would have to tell her.

His family probably thought he was dead, and there was no way he could let them know he wasn't without jeopardizing them. If his cover was blown, his family would be at risk if Piggot ever found out he hadn't died as planned. The way things stood now, he'd have a hard time convincing his family of his identity anyway; he neither looked nor sounded the same. His hands were tied until Piggot was caught; then he supposed Sabin would arrange for his family to be notified that a "mistake" had been made in identification, and due to extenuating and unusual circumstances, et cetera, the error had only now been corrected. The Man probably already had the telegram composed in his mind, letter-perfect.

His family would be taken care of; they would be glad to get him back despite the way he looked, or the fact that his voice was ruined.

Jay was the victim. They'd used her as the ultimate cover. How in hell could she ever forgive that?

Jay dozed, finally awakening as they turned onto the track to the meadow. "We're home," she murmured, pushing her hair back. She turned her head to smile at him. "At last."

He was tense again, surveying every detail of the track. There was new snow on the ground, filling the tire tracks they had made the day before and also obliterating any other trail that could have been made after they'd left. All his training was coming into play, and Lucas Stone didn't take chances. Unnecessary chances, that was. There had been more times than one when he'd laid his life on the line, but only because he'd had no other choice. Taking chances with Jay's life, however, was something else.

As usual, Jay picked up on his tension and fell silent, a worried frown puckering her brow.

The snow surrounding the cabin was pristine, but when Lucas parked the Jeep he put a detaining hand on Jay's arm. "Stay here until I check the cabin," he said tersely, drawing a pistol from beneath his jacket and getting out without looking at her. His eyes were never still, darting from window to window, examining every inch of ground, looking for the betraying flutter of a curtain.

Jay was frozen in place. This man, moving like a cat toward the back door, was the man she loved, and he was a predator, a hunter. He was innately cautious, as graceful as the wind as he flattened his back against the wall and eased his left hand toward the doorknob, while the pistol was held ready in his right. Soundlessly he opened the door and disappeared within. Two minutes later he stood in the back door again, relaxed. "Come on in," he said, and walked back to the Jeep to get their bags.

It irritated her that he'd frightened her for nothing; it reminded her of the morning when he'd tracked her in the snow. "Don't do that to me," she snapped as she threw open the door and slid out. The snow crunched under her boots.

"Do what?"

"Scare me like that."

"Scaring you is a hell of a lot better than walking into an ambush," he replied evenly.

"How could anyone know we're up here, and why should anyone care?"

"Frank thinks someone would care, or they wouldn't have taken the trouble to hide us."

She climbed the steps and knocked the snow off her boots before entering the cabin. It was cold but not icy, because they had left the backup heat system on. She took the bags from him and carried them into the bedroom to begin unpacking while he built a fire.

Lucas watched the yellow flames lick at the logs he'd placed on the grate, slowly catching and engulfing the wood. He couldn't tell her, not yet. This might be the only time he'd ever have with her, an indefinite period of grace while Sabin's men hunted Piggot. He'd use that time to bind her to him so tightly that he could hold her even after she found out his real name, and that Steve Crossfield was dead. She had told him she loved him, but it was Steve Crossfield she'd been saying the words to, and, oddly, it had been Steve Crossfield hearing them. He was Lucas Stone, and he wanted her for himself.

His need was fast and urgent, like a fire low in his belly. He walked into the bedroom and watched her for a moment as she bent over to remove her boots and socks. She was as slim as a reed, her skin silky soft. He caught her around the waist and tumbled her on the bed, immediately following her down to pin her to the mattress with his weight.

She laughed, her blue eyes no longer filled with irritation. "The caveman approach must be fashionable this year," she teased.

He couldn't smile in return. He wanted her too badly, needed to hear her say the words to *him*, not to a ghost. The yellow glitter was in his eyes as he stripped her and surveyed her nakedness. Her nipples were puckered from the chilly air, her breasts standing up round and firm. He circled them with his hands and lifted the tight nipples to his mouth, sucking at each of them in turn. She gasped, and her back arched. Her responsiveness did it to him every time, shattered his control and made him as hot and eager for her as a teenager. He could barely tolerate taking his hands off her long enough to hastily tear at his own clothing and throw it to the side.

"Tell me you love me," he said as he adjusted her slim legs around his hips and began entering her.

Jay squirmed voluptuously, rubbing her breasts against the hairy planes of his chest. "I love you." Her hands dug into his back as she felt the muscles ripple. "I love you." Slowly he pushed and slowly she accepted him, her pleasure already rising to an urgent pitch. Her body was so attuned to him that when he began the rhythmic thrust and withdrawal of lovemaking her sensual tension swiftly reached a crescendo. He held her until her shudders stilled, then found the rhythm anew.

"Again," he whispered.

She wanted to cry out his name, but couldn't. She couldn't call him Steve now, and she didn't dare call him Lucas. She had to bite her lips to keep his name unsaid, and a moan rose in her throat. He controlled her, his slow, deep thrusts taking her only so high and refusing to let her go any higher. She was on fire, her nerve endings exploding with pleasure.

"Tell me you love me." His voice was gravelly, the strain apparent on his face as he kept his movements agonizingly slow.

"I love you."

"Again."

"I love you."

He wanted to hear his name, but that was denied him. Sometime in the future, when this was all over, he promised himself that he would have her as he was having her now, and she would scream his name. He had to be content with knowing it himself, and with the way her eyes locked with his as she whispered the words over and over again, until his control broke and sweet madness claimed them both.

He couldn't get enough of her, ever, and knowing that he might lose her was intolerable. Physical bonds were the most basic, and instinctively he used them to strengthen the link between them. He would make himself a part of her until his name no longer mattered.

Two nights later, Frank had just gotten into bed when the telephone rang. With a sigh, he reached for it. "Payne."

"Piggot's in Mexico City," the Man said.

Forgetting about the good night's sleep he'd been anticipating, Frank sat up, instantly alert.

"Do you have a man on him?"

"Not at the moment. He's gone to ground again. It's about to unravel, and this move tells me who snipped the thread. I'll take care of that little detail, but you get Luke out of there. The cabin's location has been leaked."

"How much do you want me to tell him?"

"All of it. It doesn't matter now. It'll go down within the next twenty-four hours. Just see that they're safe." Then Kell Sabin hung up, wondering if he'd cut it too fine and endangered a friend, as well as an innocent woman.

Chapter Twelve

At the first beep from the palm-size pager lying on the bedside table, Lucas was on his feet and reaching for his pants. The tone told him it was the communications beeper, not the alarm caused by the laser beam being broken, but the very fact that Frank was contacting him in the middle of the night was alarm enough. Jay roused and reached for the lamp, but Lucas stopped her.

"No lights."

"What's going on?" She was very still now.

"I'm going out to the shed. That's the communications beeper. Frank's trying to get in touch with us."

"Then why not turn on a light?"

"He wouldn't contact us in the middle of the night unless it was an emergency. It might be too late. Piggot could already be close by, and a light would warn him."

"Piggot?"

"The guy who tried to make me into beef stew, remember?"

"I'll go with you." In a flash she was out of the bed and fumbling with her clothes in the dark. Lucas started to stop her, not wanting her to leave the safety of the cabin, but if Piggot had found them, the cabin wouldn't be safe. A hand-held rocket launcher in the hands of an expert, which Piggot was, could turn the cabin into a shattered inferno in seconds.

He stamped his feet into his boots and grabbed the pistol out of the holster, which he always kept at hand. As he left the room he lifted his jacket from the hook beside the door, then shrugged into it as he raced through the dark cabin to the back door. Jay was right behind him; she had on her jeans and his flannel shirt, her bare feet shoved into boots.

They slipped across the snow to the shed, staying in the shadows as much as possible. The ramshackle shed was a revelation; Jay had been stunned the first time Lucas had shown her what lay below its surface. He moved a bale of hay aside and revealed a small trapdoor, just wide enough to allow his shoulders through, then pressed a button on the pager that released the electronic lock. The trapdoor silently swung open. A narrow ladder extended downward, illuminated only by tiny red lights beside each step. Lucas urged her down, then he followed and closed the door, once more sealing the underground communications chamber. Only then did he switch on the lights.

The chamber was small, no more than six by eight, and crammed with equipment. There were a computer and display terminal, a modem hookup and a printer against the end wall, and an elaborate radio system on the right. That left about two and a half feet of room on the left for maneuvering, and part of that was taken up by a chair. Lucas took the chair and flipped switches on the radio. "On air."

"Get packed. Piggot has been spotted in Mexico City, and we have word the location of the cabin is no longer secure." Frank's voice filled the small chamber eerily, without the tinny sound radios normally produced, testifying to the quality of the set.

"How much time do we have?"

"The Man estimated four hours; less if Piggot has already put accomplices in the area."

"His usual method is to move people in, but keep them at a distance until he arrives. He likes to orchestrate things himself." Lucas's voice was remote, his mind racing.

Silence filled the chamber, then Frank asked quietly, "Luke?"

"Yeah," Lucas said, aware of Jay's sudden movement behind him, followed by absolute stillness. He hadn't wanted to tell her like this, but all hell would be coming down in a hurry. Four hours wasn't a lot of time, and no matter what happened, he wanted her to know his name. For four hours she would know whose woman she was.

"When?"

"A couple of days ago. Any chance of intercepting Piggot before he gets here?" That would be the best-case scenario.

"Slim. Nailing him there would be our best bet. We don't know where he is, but we know where he's going."

"He won't go through customs, so that means he's in a small plane and will land at a private airstrip, one close by. Do you have a record of them?"

"We're pulling them out of the computer now. We'll have men at all of them."

"Where's a safe place for me to stash Jay?"

Frank said urgently, "Luke, you're out of it. Don't set yourself up as bait for the trap. Get in the Jeep and drive, and call me in five hours."

"Piggot's my mess, I'll clean it up," Lucas said, still in that cool, remote tone. "If I'd taken care of him last year, this wouldn't be happening now."

"What about Jay?"

"I'll get her out of it. But I'm coming back for Piggot."

Realizing the futility of arguing with him across two-thirds of the continent, Frank said. "Okay. Contact Veasey, at this frequency, and scramble." He recited the frequency numbers only once.

"Roger," Lucas said, and flipped the switch that cut them off. Then he shoved the chair back and stood, turning to face Jay.

Her entire body felt numb as she stared at him. He knew. His memory had returned. Her time of grace had ended, the mirrors had shattered, the charade was over. The violence that had brought him into her life was about to take him out of it again.

With the return of his memory, he was truly Lucas Stone again. It was there in his eyes, in the yellow gaze of the predator. His face was hard. "I'm not Steve Crossfield," he said bluntly. "My name is Lucas Stone. Your ex-husband is dead."

She was white, frozen. "I know," she whispered.

Of all the things he'd expected her to say, that wasn't one of them. It stunned him, confused him, and irrationally angered him. He'd agonized for days over how to tell her, and she already knew? "How long have you known?" he snapped.

Even her lips felt numb. "Quite a while."

He caught her arm, his long fingers digging into her flesh. "How long is 'quite a while'?"

She tried to think. She had been caught in a web of lies for so long that it was difficult to remember. "You . . . you were still in the hospital."

Scenarios flashed through his mind. He'd been trained to think deviously, to keep hammering at something until it made sense, and he didn't like any of the situations that came to mind. He'd assumed from the beginning that she was an innocent blind, used by Sabin and Frank Payne to shield him, but it was more likely that she'd been hired to do the job. White-hot fury began to build in him, and he clamped down on his temper with iron control. "Why didn't you tell me?" God, for a while he'd thought he was going crazy, with all those damn memories coming back and none of them connected with the things she had told him. He might have gotten his memory back sooner if he'd had one solid fact to build on instead of the fairy tales she'd woven.

He was hurting her; his grip would leave bruises on her arm. She pulled at it uselessly, gasping as he only tightened his fingers. "I was afraid to!"

"Afraid of what?"

"I thought Frank would send me away if he knew I'd discovered you weren't Steve! Lucas, please, you're hurting me!" At last she could say his name, even though it was in pain, and her heart savored the sound.

His grip eased, but he caught her other arm, too, and held her firmly. "So Frank didn't hire you to say I was Steve Crossfield?"

"N-no," she stuttered. "I believed you were, at first."

"What changed your mind?"

"Your eyes. When I saw your eyes, I knew."

The memory of that was crystal clear. When the doctor had cut the bandages away from his eyes and he'd looked at Jay for the first time, she had gone as white as she was now. That was odd, because he knew Sabin would never have overlooked a detail as basic as the color of his eyes.

"Your husband didn't have brown eyes?"

"Ex-husband," she whispered. "Yes, he had brown eyes, but his were dark brown. Yours are yellowish brown."

So his eyes were a different shade of brown than her husband's had been; it was almost laughable that Sabin's carefully constructed scam could have fallen apart over something as small as that. But she hadn't told them that they had the wrong man, which would have been the reasonable thing to do. She hadn't even told *him*, not then and not during the weeks when they'd been up here alone. Angry frustration made his voice as rough as gravel. "Why didn't you tell *me*? Didn't you think I'd be a little interested in who I really am?"

"I couldn't take the chance. I was afraid—" she began, pleading for understanding.

"Yeah, that's right, you were afraid the gravy train would end. Frank was paying you to stay with me, wasn't he? You were with me every day, so there was no way you could hold down a job."

"No! It isn't like that—"

"Then what is it like? Are you independently wealthy?"

"Lucas, please. No, I'm not wealthy—"

"Then how did you live during the months I was in the hospital?"

"Frank picked up the tab," she said in raw frustration. "Would you please listen to me?"

"I'm listening, honey. You just told me that Frank paid you to stay with me."

"He made it *possible* for me to stay with you! I'd lost my job—" Too late, she heard the words and knew how he would take them.

His eyes were yellow slits, his mouth a grim line of rage. "So you jumped at the chance for a cushy job. All you had to do was sit beside me every day and anything you wanted was given to you, while Frank paid your bills. This explains why you wouldn't marry me, doesn't it? You were happy to accept your 'salary,' but marrying a stranger was a little bit too much, wasn't it? Not to mention the fact that the marriage wouldn't have been legal. You saved yourself some sticky trouble by dragging up all those excuses."

"They weren't excuses. For all I knew you could have had someone who cared for you—"

"I do!" he yelled, his neck cording. "My family! They think I'm dead!"

Jay groped for control, managing to steady her voice. "I couldn't marry you until you'd gotten your memory back and knew for certain you wanted to marry me. I couldn't take advantage of you like that."

"That's a convenient scruple. It actually makes you look noble, doesn't it? Too bad. If you wanted the gravy train to keep running, you should have married me while you had the chance and just kept pretending I was Crossfield. Then, when I got my memory back, you could have been the poor victim and maybe I would have stayed with you out of guilt."

She shrank away from him, her eyes going blank. Somehow, during the long months she had spent with him, she had come to believe he loved her, though he had never said the words. He'd been so possessive, so tender and passionate. But now his memory had returned, and he couldn't have made it plainer that his absorption with her had ended. He didn't need her any longer, and he certainly wasn't going to renew his offer of marriage. It was over, and they weren't even going to part friends. The worst had happened; she had lied to him, kept his identity from him, and he would never forgive her for it. He thought she had done it just because the government had been willing to support her for as long as the charade had lasted.

He released her suddenly, as if he couldn't stand to touch her any longer, and she staggered back. Catching her balance, she turned toward the ladder. "Open the door," she said dully.

He clenched his fists, not ready to break off the argument. He didn't have all the answers he wanted, not by a long shot. But her movement recalled the need for urgency; he had to get her out of there before Piggot found them. The last thing he wanted was for Jay to be caught in the middle of a firefight.

"I'll go first," he said, and shouldered past her. He signaled the door open and climbed the ladder, the pistol ready in his hand. As soon as his head was above ground he looked cautiously in all directions, then climbed out and knelt on one knee by the hole to help Jay out. "All right, come on."

She didn't look at him as she crawled out, nor did she accept the hand he extended. He closed the trapdoor, then replaced the bale of hay over it. She started to just walk out of the shed, but he grabbed her and held her back. "Watch it!" he said in a furious whisper. "We go back the same way we came. Stay in the shadows." He led the way, and Jay followed him without a word.

He still wouldn't allow a light on in the cabin, so Jay stumbled to the bedroom and gathered a few clothes in the dark. He came into the bedroom as she took off his shirt to put on her own clothes, and after a moment of frozen embarrassment, she awkwardly turned her back while she struggled with her bra. Her hands were clumsy, and in the dark she couldn't manage to straighten the straps. Despairing of getting it on, she finally dropped it on the bed and simply pulled her sweater over her head.

Lucas watched her. Her pale breasts had gleamed in the faint light coming through the window, and in spite of his anger, his sense of betrayal and the need for haste, he wanted to go to her and pull her against him. Only a few hours before he had held her breasts in his hands and pushed them up to his avid mouth. He had made love to her until the building anticipation had bordered on agony, and they had writhed together on that bed. She had told him she loved him, over and over, and now she turned her back as if she had to hide her body from him.

It hit him hard, shook him. There was more to it than she'd told him, more than the mercenary motives he'd thrown at her. He needed to know what it was, but he didn't have time. Damn it. If only she didn't look so beaten and remote, as if she had withdrawn inside herself. He had to fight the urge to take her in his arms and kiss that look away. Hell, what did it matter why she had done it? Maybe money had been the reason at first, but he was damned certain it wasn't the reason now, or at least not all of it. Even if it had been, he thought ruthlessly, he wouldn't let her go. He'd get this settled between them as soon as he'd taken care of Piggot, but right now the most important thing was to make certain Jay was safe.

"Hurry," he urged roughly.

She sat down on the edge of the bed and jerked her boots off, quickly put on a pair of thick socks and put the boots on again. Then she got her purse and shearling jacket and said, "I'm ready."

He didn't see the need for her to get anything else, as they would come back to the cabin and pack after he'd taken care of Piggot, and he was pleased that she didn't insist on wasting time. Jay was a good partner, even though she was out of her depth.

He had to find a safe place to leave her. He doubted that Black Bull, the closest town, had a motel, but he didn't have the time to go any farther than that. He drove the Jeep at breakneck speed across the meadow, especially considering that he didn't dare risk turning on the headlights. But he had taken the possibility that he might have to do this into consideration and had walked the meadow over and over, mentally tracing the route he would take, estimating his fastest safe speed, noting all the rocks and ruts in his path. He edged so close to the tree line that branches scraped the side of the Jeep.

"I can't see," Jay said, her voice strained.

"I can." He couldn't see much, but it was enough. He had good night vision.

She held on to the door as they jolted across a hump, rattling her teeth. He'd have to turn on the headlights when they went down the mountainside, she thought; the track was only wide enough for the Jeep, with a steep drop on one side and vertical mountain on the other. Even in daylight she hardly dared to breathe until they had safely negotiated it. But when they made the turn that took them onto the track, he kept both hands on the wheel. The darkness in front of them was absolute.

Jay closed her eyes. Her own heartbeat was thundering in her ears so loudly that she couldn't hear anything else. There was nothing she could do. He had decided not to turn on the lights, to risk the drive in the dark, and nothing she could say would change his mind. His arrogant confidence in his own ability was both maddening and awesome; she would rather have walked down the mountain in ten feet of snow than risked this hair-raising drive, but he had simply decided to do it, and now he was.

She couldn't estimate how long the drive took. It seemed like hours, and finally her nerves couldn't bear the tension, and numbness settled in. She even opened her eyes. It didn't matter. If they went over the side, they would go whether her eyes were open or closed.

But then they were down and bumping across the second meadow. Suddenly he slammed on the brakes, swearing viciously. Jay saw what he saw: a set of headlights playing along the edge of the meadow in front of them. They were still safely out of range of the light, but she knew as well as he did what it meant. Piggot's men were drawing close, closing the net to wait for Piggot's arrival.

Lucas put the Jeep in reverse and backed the way he had come, keeping the Jeep at the tree line. When he reached the rear edge of the meadow he turned, taking the Jeep up the north edge. They were off the track now, and the snow tires dug in deep, spewing snow back behind them.

"Are we going around this way?"

"No. We won't be able to make it. The snow's too deep." He pulled the Jeep under some trees and got out. "Stay here," he ordered, and disappeared back toward the track.

Jay swiveled in her seat, straining her eyes to see what he was doing. She could barely make out his form, black against the snow; an instant later he was out of sight.

He was back in less than two minutes. He vaulted into the Jeep and slammed the door, then rolled the window down. "Listen," he hissed.

"What did you do?"

"I wiped out our tracks. There was only one vehicle. If it goes past us, we'll get back on the track and make it to the highway yet."

They listened. The sound of the other motor came plainly through the night air. The vehicle was moving slowly, the engine toiling in low gear as it cautiously made its way up the slick, snowy, unfamiliar track. The headlights stabbed the darkness, coming almost straight toward them.

"Don't worry," Lucas breathed. "They can't see us from the track. If they just don't notice where we turned and if they keep on going, we'll be okay."

Two ifs. Two big ifs. Jay's nails were digging into her palms. The headlights were close enough that their reflected light illuminated the interior of the Jeep, and for the first time she noticed that Lucas had on his thick shearling jacket, but no shirt. The odd detail struck her, and she wondered if she might be edging toward hysteria.

"Keep going," he said under his breath. "Keep going."

For a moment it seemed as if the other vehicle slowed, and the lights seemed to be coming over the slight rise straight toward them. Then they turned, and the noise of the engine slowly moved away.

She let out her breath. Lucas started the engine, knowing the sound wouldn't be heard over that of the other motor. He put the Jeep in gear and turned it around, praying they were hidden well enough that the red glow of the brake lights wouldn't reveal their position. But at least they were behind the other vehicle now. If he had to, he could make a run for the road. As rough as the track was, the chance that they would be hit by gunfire from a pursuing vehicle was small.

The Jeep lurched through the snow, and then they were on the track again. No other headlights disturbed the darkness, and they could just catch glimpses of light playing through the trees as the other vehicle moved slowly up the treacherous mountainside track.

Jay sat silently, even when they reached the road and Lucas finally turned on the headlights. She was numb again.

They reached Black Bull at two in the morning. The local populace of one hundred and thirty-three souls were all in bed. There wasn't even an all-night convenience store, and the one gas station closed at ten at night, according to the sign in the window. A county sheriff's car was parked at the side of the gas station.

Lucas stopped the Jeep. "Can you drive this well enough to get out of here?" he asked brusquely.

She looked at the gearshift, but not at him. "Yes."

"Then drive until you hit the next town big enough to have a motel. Stop there and call Frank. He'll arrange for you to be picked up. Do you have his number?"

So this was it. It was over. "No."

"Give me a pen. I'll write it down for you."

Jay fumbled in her purse and found a pen, but she didn't have even a scrap of paper for him to write the number on. Finally he grasped her hand and turned it palm up, then wrote the number on her palm.

"Where are you going?" she asked, her voice strained but even.

"I'm taking that county car right there and radioing Veasey. Then we're going to catch Piggot and end this once and for all."

She stared out the windshield, her hand clenched tightly as if to keep the number from fading off her palm. "Be careful," she managed to say, the admonishment trite but heartfelt. She wondered if Frank would even tell her the outcome, if she would ever know what happened to Lucas.

"He ambushed me once. It won't happen again." Lucas got out of the Jeep and strode over to the county car. It was locked, but that wasn't much of a deterrent. He had the door open in less than ten seconds. He looked at the Jeep, staring at Jay through the windshield. Her face was ghostly white. He wanted nothing more than to jerk her into his arms and kiss her so hard that they both forgot about this mess, but if he kissed her now, he might not be able to stop, and he had to take care of Piggot. It was just that he wanted her so badly, wanted to use the bond of the flesh to make certain she knew she was his. A sense of incompletion gnawed at him because they hadn't thrashed out the situation between them, but it would have to wait. Maybe it was better this way. In a few hours he wouldn't have to worry about Piggot any longer, and his temper would have cooled. He would be able to think clearly and not react as if she'd betrayed him. He didn't understand her reasons yet, but underneath everything, he knew she loved him.

Instead of climbing over into the driver's seat, Jay opened the door and got out to walk around. She paused in front of the Jeep, her slim body starkly outlined by the glare of the headlights. "It was the only way I could think of to protect you," she said, then got into the Jeep and put it in gear.

Lucas watched the taillights as she pulled out of the gas station and onto the highway. He felt stunned. Protect him? He was so used to being out in the cold, on his own by choice, that the idea of anyone protecting him was alien. What had she thought she could do?

She could keep the charade intact. She had been right; Frank would have quickly and quietly hustled her away if she'd told him there had been a mistake, that he, Lucas, wasn't her ex-husband. She didn't have his skill with weapons or in fighting, but that hadn't stopped her from literally setting herself up as his bodyguard. The charade had depended on her, so she had kept quiet, and shielded him with her presence.

Because she loved him. He swore aloud, his breath crystallizing in the frigid night air. His damned training had tripped him up, making him look for betrayal where there hadn't been any, making him question her motives and automatically assuming the worst. He had only to look to himself to understand why she hadn't said anything. Hadn't he kept quiet these past two days because he'd been afraid of losing her if she knew the truth? He loved her too much to accept even the possibility of losing her, until Piggot had forced his hand.

Swearing again, he folded his length into the county car and began the process of hot-wiring the starter.

* * *

Dawn threw rosy fingers of light across the snow, a sight Lucas has seen many times since coming to the mountains, but the scene wasn't peaceful this particular morning. The meadow was crowded with men and vehicles, the pristine snow trampled and criss-crossed by both feet and tires. Here and there the white was marred by reddish-brown stains. A helicopter sat off to the left, its blades slowly twirling in the breeze.

Ten guns snapped toward him as he stepped out from the trees, then were lifted as the men holding them recognized him. He walked steadily toward them, his own pistol held in his blood-stained hand down at his side. The stench of cordite burned his nostrils in the cold air, and a gray haze lay over the meadow, resisting the efforts of the breeze to disperse it.

There was a tall, black-haired man standing next to the helicopter, surveying the scene with grim, narrowed eyes. Lucas walked straight to him. "You took a chance, setting us up in your own cabin," he snapped.

Kell Sabin looked around the meadow. "It was a calculated risk. I had to do it to find the mole. Once the location of the cabin was leaked, I knew who it was, because access to that information is very controlled." He shrugged. "I can find another vacation spot."

"The mole blew my cover?"

"Yeah. Until then, I had no idea he was there." Sabin's voice was icy, his eyes like cold black fire.

"So why the masquerade? Why drag Jay into it?"

"To keep Piggot from finding out you were alive. Your cover was blown. He knew about your family, and he's been willing in the past to use someone's family to get to them. I was trying to buy time, to keep everyone safe until Piggot surfaced and we could get to him."

Sabin looked up at the trees behind the cabin. "I assume he won't be bothering us again."

"Or anyone else."

"That was your last job. You're out of it."

"Damn straight," Lucas agreed. "I've got better things to do, like get married and start a family."

Suddenly Sabin grinned, and the coldness left his eyes. Few people saw Sabin like that, only the ones who could call themselves his friends. "The bigger they are," he jibed, and left the rest of the old saw unsaid. "Have you told her yet?"

"She already knew. She figured it out while I was still in the hospital."

Sabin frowned. "What? She didn't say anything. How did she know?"

"My eyes. They're a different shade of brown than Crossfield's."

"Hell. A little thing like that. And she still went along with it?"

"I think she figured out that the whole thing was to protect me."

"Women," Sabin said softly, thinking of his own wife, who had fought like a tigress to save his life when he'd been a stranger to her. It didn't surprise him that Jay Granger had put herself on the line to protect Lucas.

Lucas rubbed his jaw. "She doesn't even mind this ugly mug."

"The surgeons did what they could. Your face was smashed." Then Sabin grinned again. "You were too pretty anyway."

The two men stood and watched the mopping up process, their faces becoming grim again at the loss of life. Three men were dead, counting Piggot, and four more were in custody. "I'll notify your family that you're alive," Sabin finally said. "I'm sorry they had to go through this, but with Piggot on the loose, it was safer for you, and all of them, as well, if the charade was played out. It's over now. Collect Jay from wherever you've stashed her, and we'll get the two of you out of here."

Lucas looked at him, and slowly the blood drained out of his face. "She hasn't called Frank?" he asked hoarsely.

Sabin went still. "No. Where is she?"

"She was supposed to drive to the next town, check into a motel and call Frank. Damn it to hell!" Lucas turned and ran for the shed, with Sabin right beside him. Suddenly he felt cold all over. There was a possibility Piggot could have gotten to Jay before coming here, as well as the slightly less terrifying possibility that she could have had an accident. God in heaven, where was she?

After leaving Lucas, Jay simply drove, automatically following the highway signs picked out by the headlight beams, and eventually wound up on U.S. 24, the highway that they had taken to Colorado Springs. She turned in the opposite direction. She didn't pay any attention to the time; she just kept driving. U.S. 24 took her through Leadville, and finally she connected with I-70. She took a right, toward Denver.

The sun came up, shining right into her eyes. She was nearly out of gas. She got off at the next exit and had the tank filled.

It would be over by now.

Exhaustion pulled at her, but she couldn't stop. If she ever stopped, she would have to think, and right now she couldn't bear it. She checked her money. She didn't have much—a little over sixty dollars—but she had her credit cards. That would get her back to New York, to the only home she had left, the only refuge.

I-70 went straight to Stapleton International Airport in Denver. Jay parked the Jeep and entered the terminal, carefully noting where she had parked so she could tell Frank where to retrieve his vehicle. She bought her ticket first, and was lucky enough to get on a flight leaving within the hour. Then she found a pay phone and called Frank.

He answered in the middle of the first ring. "Frank, it's Jay." She identified herself in a numb monotone. "Is it over?"

"Where the hell are you?" he screamed.

"Denver."

"Denver! What are you doing there? You were supposed to call me hours ago! Luke is tearing the damned place up, and we have every cop in Colorado prowling the highways looking for you."

Her heart lightened, the terrible dread lifting from it. "He's all right? He isn't hurt?"

"He's fine. He took a little nick on the arm, but nothing a Band-Aid won't cover. Look, exactly where are you? I'll have you picked up—"

"Is it over?" she asked insistently. "Is it really over?"

"Piggot? Yeah, it's over. Luke got him. Tell me where you are and—"

"I'm glad." Her legs wouldn't support her much longer; she sagged against the wall. "Take . . . take care of him."

"My God, don't hang up!" Frank yelled, the words shrieking in her ear. "Where are you?"

"Don't worry," she managed to say. "I can get home by myself." Totally forgetting the Jeep, she hung up the phone, then went into the ladies' rest room and splashed cold water on her face. As she pulled a brush through her hair she noticed the pallor of her cheeks and the dark circles under her eyes. "You guys sure know how to show a lady a good time," she murmured to her reflection, drawing several startled glances her way.

Yogi Berra had said, "It ain't over till it's over," but this was very definitely over. Jay couldn't sleep on the flight, despite the utter exhaustion weighing down her body. Nor could she eat, though her stomach was empty. She managed to drink a cola, but nothing more.

After the solitude of the meadow, New York's J.F.K. airport was bedlam. She wanted to shrink against a wall and scream at all the scurrying people to go away. Instead she got on a bus, and an hour and a half later she let herself into her apartment.

She hadn't seen it in months; it was no longer home. It had been well taken care of in her absence, as Frank had promised, but it was as empty as she was. She didn't even have any clothes with her. She laughed hollowly; clothes were the least of her worries. Frank would make certain they were shipped to her.

But there were sheets to go on the bed, and towels for the bathroom. She took a warm shower, then even summoned the strength to make up the bed. The afternoon sun was going down as she stretched out naked between the clean sheets. Automatically she turned, searching for Lucas's warmth, but he wasn't there. It was over, and he didn't want her. Acid tears stung her eyes as her heavy eyelids closed, and then she slept.

"Janet Jean. Janet Jean, wake up."

The intruding voice pulled her toward consciousness. She didn't want to wake up. So long as she slept, she didn't have to face life without Lucas. But it sounded like his voice, and she frowned.

"Janet Jean. Jay. Wake up, baby." A hard, warm hand shook her bare shoulder.

Slowly she opened her eyes. It *was* Lucas, sitting on the edge of her bed, scowling at her. Those yellow eyes looked almost murderous, though his tone had been as gentle as his ruined voice would allow. He looked like hell; he badly needed a shave, his hair was uncombed, and a bloodstained bandage was wrapped around his left forearm. But at least he had on a shirt now, and his clothes were clean.

"I know I locked the door." Sleep still muddled her mind, but she knew she'd locked the door. In New York, one wasn't careless about locking the door.

He shrugged. "Big deal. Come on, sweetheart, go to the bathroom and splash some cold water on your face so you can focus your eyes. I'll make coffee."

What was he doing here? She couldn't think of any reason, and though part of her rejoiced at seeing him, no matter why, another part of her cringed at having to say goodbye to him again. She might not be able to stand it this time. At least before, she had been numb.

"What time is it?"

"Almost nine."

"It can't be. It's still daylight."

"Nine in the morning," he explained patiently. "Come on, get up." He lifted her to a sitting position, and the covers fell to her waist, exposing her bare body. Quickly Jay grabbed the sheet and pulled it over her breasts; she couldn't meet his eyes as a flush chased the pallor from her face.

His face was expressionless as he got to his feet and unbuttoned his shirt. "Here, put this on. I packed your clothes and brought them with me, but they're all tumbled together in the suitcases."

She took his shirt, still warm from his body, and pulled it around her. Without another word she got up and went into the bathroom, firmly closing the door behind her. She started to lock it, but decided not to waste her time. Locks weren't much good against him.

Five minutes later she felt much more alert, having followed his advice and splashed cold water on her face. She was very thirsty, after having gone so long without anything to drink, so she drank several cups of water. She would have felt more secure if she'd had on something more than just his shirt, but it almost swallowed her. His scent was on the fabric. She lifted it to her face and inhaled deeply, then let it drop and left the security of the bathroom.

He was lying on the bed. She stopped in her tracks. "I thought you were going to make coffee."

"You don't have any." He got to his feet, put his hands on her shoulders and shook her. "Damn you," he said in a shaking voice. "I went through hell when I found out you hadn't called Frank. Why did you run? Why did you come back here?"

Her hair had fallen over her face. "I didn't have anyplace else to go," she said, and her voice cracked.

He yanked her into his arms, reaching up behind her back to lock his fist in her hair and hold her head back. "Did you really think I'd let you get away from me that easily?" he all but snarled.

"Was what I did so bad?" she pleaded. "I didn't know any other way to protect you! When I saw your eyes, I knew you had to be the agent Frank had told me had been killed, and I knew he'd gone to an awful lot of trouble to hide you, so you had to be in danger. You had amnesia. You didn't even know who was after you! Keeping the lie going was the only way I had of keeping you safe!''

The yellowish eyes glittered. ''Why should you care?''

''Because I was in love with you! Or did you think that was a lie, too?''

His touch gentled. ''No,'' he said quietly. ''I think I've always known you loved me, right from the start.''

Tears leaked from the corners of her eyes. ''The first time I touched you,'' she whispered, ''I felt how warm you were, and how hard you were fighting to stay alive. I started loving you then.''

''Then why did you run?''

He was relentless, but then, she had always known that. ''Because it was over. You didn't want me. I'd been terrified of what you would do when you found out. I was afraid you'd send me away, and you did. So I left.''

''I only wanted you away from the danger, damn it! I didn't intend for you to go two thousand miles!'' He picked her up and dropped her on the bed, then followed her down. ''No excuses this time. We're going to get married as soon as we can legally do it.''

She was as stunned as she had been the first time he'd mentioned marriage. ''W-what?'' she stammered.

''You told me to ask you again when I'd regained my memory. Well, I have. We're getting married.''

All she could say was, ''That's not asking, that's telling.''

''It'll do.'' He began unbuttoning his shirt, uncovering her breasts.

"Is it because you think you owe me—"

His head jerked up, those eyes fierce and wild. "I love you so much I'm out of my head with it."

She was stunned again. "You never said. I thought—but then you made me leave..."

"I didn't think I could have made it any plainer how I felt," he growled.

Very simply she said, "Do you need the words?"

That stopped him. "I need the words very much."

"So do I."

He bent his head and kissed her, his hand stroking her bare body beneath the shirt. His muscled legs moved against hers, and she felt his hardness against her thigh. "I love you, Jay Granger."

The sun was exploding inside her, lighting her eyes. "I love you, Lucas Stone."

At last she could speak his name with love.

Epilogue

Is Piggot really dead?"

"He's really dead." Lucas watched her face carefully across the breakfast table. He had gone out and bought the necessary groceries, and they had both eaten as if they were starved, which they had been. He hadn't been interested in food before, either. Finding Jay and getting her back where she belonged had been far more important. "I finished the job." The truth wasn't pretty, but she had a right to know that about the man she was going to marry.

She sipped at the hot coffee, then lifted those incredible dark blue eyes to his. "I'm glad he's dead," she said fiercely. "He tried to kill you."

"And came damn close to succeeding."

She shuddered, thinking of the days when his life had hung in the balance, and he reached for her hand. "Hey, sweetheart. It's over. That part is really over.

This part—" he squeezed her hand "—is just getting started—if you're sure you can stand looking at this face over the breakfast table."

The smile broke over her face like sunshine. "Well, you're not good-looking, but you sure are sexy."

With a growl he grabbed for her, dragging her around the table and onto his lap. Her arms went around him even as he tilted her face up for his kiss. "By the way, I'm not an agent."

She jerked back, startled. "What?"

"Not any longer. I'm officially retired, as of yesterday. Sabin took me out of it. Once my cover was blown, there was no way I could go back without endangering my family. I've really been out of it since the explosion, but Sabin didn't make it official until Piggot was caught."

"Then I guess we'll both have to hunt for a job." He was retired! She felt like chanting hosannas. She wouldn't have to worry every time he walked out the door that she'd never see him again.

He rubbed his thumb over her bottom lip. "I already have a job, baby. I'm a businessman, in partnership with my brother in an engineering firm. I traveled all over the world. It was a good cover for the work I was doing for Sabin. Speaking of my brother, by now Sabin will have gotten the news to them that a mistake was made in identifying the victims of the explosion and I'm still alive. This is going to be a bad shock to them, especially my parents."

"You mean a good shock."

"It'll be a shock, of whatever nature. Given the changes in my face and voice, they may have trouble adjusting."

"And you're bringing a strange woman into the family," she said, concern darkening her eyes.

"Oh, that. Don't worry about that. Mom has been after me for years to settle down. It wasn't an option I had before, but that's changed." He gave her a raffish grin. "I'd already decided to retire, anyway, so I could spend my time keeping you satisfied."

He certainly did that. Jay put her head on his shoulder, absorbing his warmth and nearness. His arms tightened. "I love you," he said steadily.

"I love you, Lucas Stone." She would never tire of saying it, and he would never tire of hearing it.

He stood up with her in his arms. "Let's go make a phone call. I want to talk to my folks and let them know they're getting a daughter-in-law."

They did make the phone call, but not right away. First he kissed her, and when he lifted his head the expression in his eyes had intensified. He carried her into the bedroom, and then the mirror on the wall reflected the true image of two people entwined as they loved each other.

* * * * *

ATTRACTIVE, SPACE SAVING BOOK RACK

Display your most prized novels on this handsome and sturdy book rack. The hand-rubbed walnut finish will blend into your library decor with quiet elegance, providing a practical organizer for your favorite hard-or softcovered books.

Only $9.95

Approximately 16" x 8" when assembled

Assembles in seconds!

To order, rush your name, address and zip code, along with a check or money order for $10.70* ($9.95 plus 75¢ postage and handling) payable to *Silhouette Books*.

Silhouette Books
Book Rack Offer
901 Fuhrmann Blvd.
P.O. Box 1396
Buffalo, NY 14269-1396

Offer not available in Canada.

BKR-2A

*New York and Iowa residents add appropriate sales tax.

Silhouette Special Edition

**In May, Silhouette SPECIAL EDITION
shoots for the stars with six heavenly romances
by a stellar cast of Silhouette favorites....**

Nora Roberts
celebrates a golden anniversary—her 50th Silhouette
novel—and launches a delightful new family series, THE
O'HURLEYS! with *THE LAST HONEST WOMAN* (#451)

Linda Howard
weaves a delicious web of FBI deceit—and slightly embellished
"home truths"—in *WHITE LIES** (#452)

Tracy Sinclair
whisks us to Rome, where the jet set is rocked by a cat
burglar—and a woman is shocked by a thief of hearts—in
MORE PRECIOUS THAN JEWELS (#453)

Curtiss Ann Matlock
plumbs the very depths of love as an errant husband attempts
to mend his tattered marriage, in *WELLSPRING* (#454)

Jo Ann Algermissen
gives new meaning to "labor of love" and "Special Delivery"
in her modern medical marvel *BLUE EMERALDS* (#455)

Emilie Richards
sets pulses racing as a traditional Southern widow tries to run
from romance California-style, in *A CLASSIC ENCOUNTER*
(#456)

**Don't miss this dazzling constellation of romance stars in
May—Only in Silhouette SPECIAL EDITION!**

*previously advertised as *MIRRORS*

Patricia Matthews, America's most beloved romance novelist and author of sixteen national bestsellers, has written a novel of compelling romantic suspense.

Patricia Matthews
Mirrors

After a young woman discovers she is to inherit an enormous family fortune, her identical twin sister stops at nothing—even murder—to assume her sister's identity and become sole heiress.

WORLDWIDE LIBRARY

MIR-1R

Silhouette Special Edition

WHITE LIES

You don't argue with the FBI. So when
they summoned Jay to identify her
gravely injured, heavily bandaged
ex-husband, she agreed to keep a
bedside vigil.

Strangely, even unconscious, Steve
wasn't at all like the husband she
remembered. As he struggled toward
awareness, he demonstrated a strength
of character, a manly power, the old
Steve had lacked. Ironically, she was
more drawn to him than ever.

When Steve finally awoke, Jay had a
unique chance to recapture—and even
embellish—the past. But would the new
Steve ever share her cherished memories?

*America's Publisher
of Contemporary Romance*

ISBN 0-373-09452-3

09452

0

65373 00275